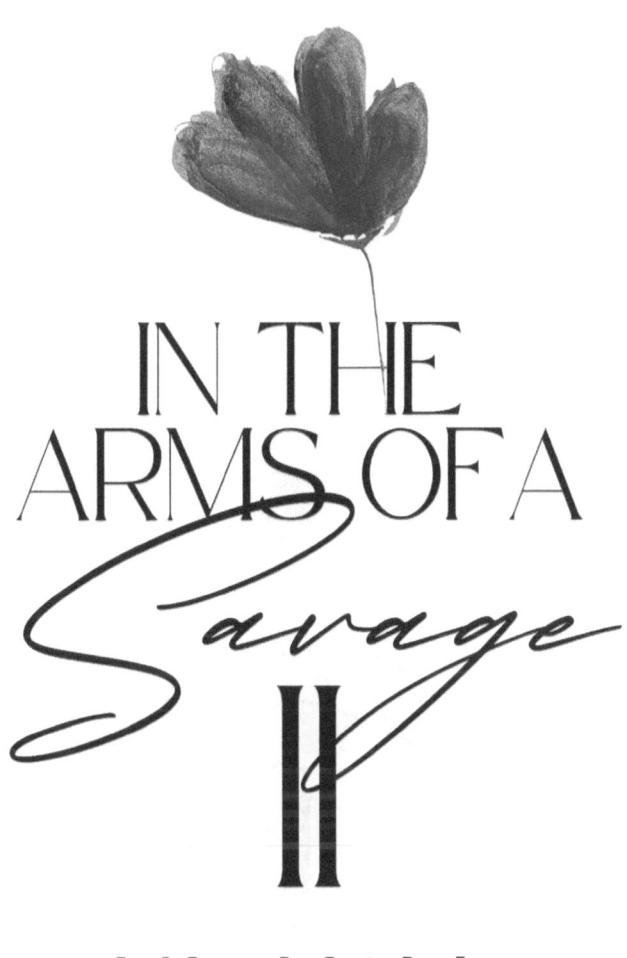

IN THE ARMS OF A
Savage
II

K.L. HALL

IN THE ARMS OF A
Savage
II

K.L. HALL

Dedication

To my godfather, William J. Brown.
"A godfather is a treasure whose worth you cannot measure except by the love in your heart."
-K.L. Hall

Acknowledgments

THANK YOU!

Oh my gosh! The release of *In the Arms of a Savage* became an Amazon #1 Best Seller in Women's Fiction and held down the number one spot for weeks! I just want to take a minute and thank each and every last one of you who took the time to purchase my book. Y'all don't understand, it took me fifteen tries to get to that #1 spot. That's fifteen books and countless hours of hard work. There were times where I wanted to give up, put the pen down, and pursue something different, but I didn't. I kept pushing forward. Yeah, over the past four years I've been in this game, I've been slept on and pushed to the side, but I kept going. This just goes to show you that anything and everything is possible if you keep grinding and keep pushing forward. Sheesh, I'm getting excited all over again just thinking about it!

Anyway, I would like to thank my Lord and Savior, Jesus Christ, because without him, nothing I do would be possible. To my family, friends, and extended family, thank you for your continuous support and always being the loudest people cheering for me in the stands. To my Royalty pen sisters and brothers, I thank you all from the bottom of my heart for your support and kind words of encouragement and empowerment. Lastly, to my readers, the OG's and the newbies, thank you so much for taking the time to read, review, and spread the word about *In the Arms of a Savage*. I hope you all enjoy this next installment as much as you did the first if not more.

All my love,
K.L. Hall

Synopsis

Raquel has always been one to play by the rules, but after her first taste of hood love, she drops her old life without a second thought, including her friends and the ashes of her last failed relationship. When her ex-fiancé comes to Miami for answers, she'll be forced to answer questions about her new life. What will she do now that she's given her heart away to Law? She knows the savage in him cannot be tamed, and it will only be a matter of time before he's out for blood.

The most valuable lesson Law ever learned wasn't from his parents but from the streets: whatever comes your way, face it on your feet. Now, he finds himself locked up with the odds stacked against him. He knows his setup wasn't random but by design. All roads lead to Shiya. Thanks to her, he may have to clean up the mess his brother created, even if that means doing a bid for a trigger he didn't pull. As he prepares to fight his case, Law becomes a menace on the streets of Miami and shows his enemies exactly how he got his name.

This love story is dripping with lies, bloodshed, and secrets, some dating back over two decades. As the boundaries between love and hate blur, it becomes harder for everyone to tell who their true enemies are. In the end, you'll witness whether Miami's new favorite couple has the strength to endure the storm.

Epigraph

"She realized that home wasn't a place. It was here, safe in his arms
..."

CHAPTER ONE

Raquel

J ay-Z said it best—Once a good girl goes bad, she's gone forever. That was the best way to describe me and the new life I was living. Before Law, I had always been the one to play by the rules, always crossing my T's and dotting my I's. I knew I had made a lot of irrational decisions, including dropping my friends and the ashes of my failed relationship with Derrick without so much as a second though. But for some reason, I didn't care. I had come to the realization that I was in love with a bad boy, and the only person in the world I cared about other than myself was Law.

I could hear the sirens blaring in my ears. Everything around me seemed to be going in slow motion. I watched as the officer placed Law in handcuffs while he was still wearing the tuxedo from his wedding with Shiya that never happened. They took his gun out of the back of his pants and handed it over to another group of officers who were smiling like they'd just won the jackpot. He was then marched over to the police car by the officer who cuffed him. He placed his hand on the top of Law's head and lowered him inside. Law didn't fight, he didn't scream, and he didn't cuss. All he did was flash me an apologetic smile as the police car sped off down the highway.

The police officer who restrained me finally let me go once Law's car was gone and another officer with a dark suit walked up to me.

"Hello. I'm Detective Shawn Mason, and you are?" he asked as he extended his hand for me to shake.

I stared down at his hand and then looked back up at his face. Once he realized I wasn't going to take the bait, he rescinded his hand.

"I'm from a special cold case unit here in Miami, and I'd like to ask you some questions if you don't mind coming down to the station, or we could do it here. It's up to you."

"I don't know anything," I said, shaking my head.

"You haven't even heard my first question."

"Look, Detective. With all due respect, it doesn't matter what you ask me because I don't know anything."

"So what's the story behind you and Andreas? High school sweethearts perhaps?"

"Do we look like we went to high school together?" I asked.

"I don't know. Did you?"

"No. We didn't," I said with an attitude in my tone.

"How about we start with the night you first met Mr. Calloway then?"

"What about it?"

"Where did the two of you meet?"

"I don't remember." I shrugged.

"You don't remember, huh?"

"No. I don't. Look, am I under arrest or something? If not, I'd really like to go on about my business," I told him.

Detective Mason sighed and then shifted his weight from one leg to the other.

"So, I see you're not into the cat and mouse game, and to be honest, neither am I, so I'll just get down to it. No, you're not under arrest, but we have the security footage of you running barefoot out of the same hotel where Mr. Damien Price was murdered, Miss Valentine."

My eyes widened, and I shook my head.

"What's your point? I'm sure people walk around barefoot in Miami all the time. You do know this is the beach, right?"

"And you know that there is a GPS tracking device in every smartphone, and the last location we traced yours to was at a warehouse in North Miami."

When I didn't reply, the detective spoke up again.

"This is your opportunity to give me your side of the story and tell me what happened in your own words before I start piecing the story together myself."

"My phone was stolen." I shrugged. "I don't know what else you want me to tell you."

"You know what, Miss Valentine? I don't really need you to talk at this point. I'm going to continue building a case against Mr. Calloway with or without your help. I know he had something to do with the murder of Damien Price that night."

He reached in his jacket pocket and pulled out his business card.

"Take it. You just may need it if you ever decide you want to remember something," he said.

I took the card out of his hand, and he walked away. If I'd learned anything from Law, it was to keep my mouth shut. I couldn't believe the nerve of that detective though. I sighed and put my head in my hands. From the police to the arrest, everything pointed to Shiya as far as I was concerned. I knew after Law called off the wedding, Shiya would be out for blood, but I never thought she'd flip on Law the way she did. That told me the one thing that I already knew, that hoe wasn't loyal from the start.

* * *

Ian

In the end, everyone has to pay for their sins. I had done a lot of fucked up shit in my life, but if the cops or any other mothafucka thought I was just gonna sit in jail and be quiet, they were out of their fucking minds. For times like the one I was in, I kept a lawyer on retainer so I wasn't too worried about anything the police _thought_ they had on me. I hated leaving Raquel the way I did, but it would be no time before I made my way back to her and made everything right between us. In the meantime, I had to play with the cards I'd been dealt.

Once we pulled up to the police station, I was pulled out of the car and shoved into the interrogation room to be questioned. If there was one thing I hated, it was the fucking police. They didn't show no love to a nigga whatsoever. They didn't give a fuck what happened to me The officer pushed me down in the chair, uncuffed my hands from behind my back, and cuffed my wrists back together in front of me so that I could rest them on the table. As soon as he walked out, a man in a suit walked in.

"Hello, Mr. Calloway. I'm Detective Shawn Mason from the special cold case unit here in Miami, and I'm here to ask you some questions."

"Let me start by asking you one first. Why was I arrested in the first place, and why the fuck am I sitting here with you right now?" I asked.

I watched the detective sit down across from me at the steel table.

"Today was supposed to be one of the happiest days of your life, right? So if you don't mind me asking, why didn't you get married today, Mr. Calloway?"

"I don't see what that has to do with shit," I shrugged.

"I already talked to Miss Valentine, Andreas. She told me everything I needed to know to build my case against you for the murder of Damien Price."

He threw a manila folder on the table and opened it. Inside were photos of Damien's dead body. I scoffed and shook my head. I could call his bluff from a mile away.

"You must think I'm fucking stupid," I told him.

"Careless maybe... but not stupid. We have the security footage of Miss Valentine running out of the hotel barefoot the night of Damien's murder. The same hotel that I bet I can pin you at around the same time Mr. Price was murdered."

"I don't know nothin' about that," I said, shaking my head.

"Okay. Well, maybe you know something about the smartphone of Miss Valentine's that we traced to a warehouse in North Miami."

"Like I said, I don't know nothin' about that shit, man, and I'm not answering shit else without my lawyer present."

"Oh, of course, guys like you always have a lawyer who's just a phone call away, huh?" he scoffed.

I stared at him like he was crazy. He was out of his mind if he thought I was going to flip at the drop of a dime. As far as I was concerned, all he did was show me his hand because I was never going to show him mine. At the end of the day, I knew what it was, and I didn't kill Damien's ass, so that shit wasn't on my conscience. If it came down to me having to do the time in order for Blaze to stay out of jail, then I'd do it in a heartbeat with no questions asked.

"Are we done here?" I asked as I adjusted my slouched posture in my seat. "I've gotta go call my lawyer."

"Oh, we're far from being done, Mr. Calloway. You better believe that."

I watched the detective push himself away from the table, grab his bullshit file, and slam the steel chair against the back wall. It took everything in me not to laugh at his corny ass. I didn't know what kind of snitches he'd been dealing with over the course of his career, but he'd met his match as far as I was concerned. Once he left, I was escorted to the nearest pay phone to call my lawyer.

"Clifton speaking," he answered.

"Yo, Clifton, it's me, Andreas."

"Andreas? What's going on? Are you calling me from jail?"

"Yeah, they tryna lock me up for some shit I didn't do, so I need you to get down here and find out what you can about what they're trying to charge me with and how much it's gonna cost for me to get out this bitch. I got shit to do."

"Okay, just hang tight. I'll be down there as soon as I can. Just don't talk to anybody."

"They already tried me with this one detective who sounds like he's got it out for me. I need you to look into him, too. Somethin' ain't right about his ass," I mumbled.

"Don't say anything else, I'll handle it all. Sit tight and I'll see you soon," he told me.

"Aight," I said and ended the call.

Nobody had to tell me that what happened to me was a setup because I already knew what it was. The entire thing had Shiya's snake ass name written all over it. If that was her way of getting back at me for calling off the wedding, then she wasn't going to want to see my ass coming. I couldn't wait to get out of jail and teach her ass a lesson that she'd never fucking forget.

Blaze

I couldn't believe that Law had shut Nashiya down the way he did at their wedding. My brother was cold for that one, but she had it coming. Like I said from the beginning, I never really had a problem with her. I just knew she wasn't right for a nigga like Law plain and simple. After Shiya ran out of the church, I walked out with the rest of the guests to give Law some space when my phone vibrated inside my pocket.

"Hello?"

"Baby boy," my mother said on the other end.

"What's up, Mom? Everything okay?"

"I'm surprised you answered. Ain't today your brother's wedding?" she asked with an attitude in her tone.

I chuckled. My mother couldn't stand Shiya, and everybody knew it. She hated her so much that she refused to come to the wedding even after we all begged her to. She didn't really leave the house too often, and she didn't see her middle son's wedding as an important reason to change her ways. She'd been laying low ever since our father was killed.

"You don't have to worry about none of that anymore, Ma."

"What do you mean? Did he do it? Is he married?"

"No. It didn't happen. He didn't go through with it," I told her.

My mother sighed into the phone.

"Good. Now I wish I would've came." She chuckled and then coughed.

"You alright, Ma?"

"When are you going to settle down?" she asked, ignoring my question.

"C'mon, Ma. You know I can't be tamed. Never could be. You okay though?" I asked for a second time.

"Baby boy ..."

"Yeah?"

"I need you to do something for me."

"What is it?"

"I need you to come see me. There's... there's something I need to tell you, but you cannot tell your brother."

"What? What do you mean I can't tell him? What's going on?"

"Are you coming or not?" she asked as she cleared her throat.

"Okay. I'm on my way," I said and hung up.

I looked back at the church and then headed to my car. I figured Raquel would find a ride home with my brother. I hopped into my ride and tossed my phone into the passenger seat. I loosened my bow tie and unbuttoned my cufflinks. My tires spun as I pulled out of the church's parking lot blasting Rick Ross's *Rather You Than Me* album.

When I pulled up to my mother's house, I immediately got a warm feeling inside. It felt like home. I shut the engine off and walked up to the front door to knock.

"It's open," I heard my mother say from inside the house.

I walked into the house and looked around.

"Ma? Where you at!" I yelled.

"Living room," she replied.

I walked into the kitchen and opened up the refrigerator to grab something to eat. I grabbed an apple off the countertop and then made my way into the living room.

"Hey, Ma. You need to get some groceries up in here. That's

the barest I've ever seen the fridge in like... well... ever," I said as I flopped down on the couch and bit into the apple.

"I haven't had much of an appetite lately."

I looked over at her and did a double take. I barely recognized the woman sitting across from me. She didn't look like my mother at all. Her once youthful, bronze skin had an ash-gray tone. Her body looked as if she hadn't eaten a real meal in a few days, maybe even a week or so. She wore a Miami Dolphin baseball cap to hide her hair and a pair of black sweatpants that were hanging loosely off her small frame.

"Ma, what's going on with you? Why you don't look like yourself?"

"Because I'm not myself, and that's what I wanted to talk to you about."

"What's going on? You got a cold or something? Have you been to the doctor? You need me to take you or something?"

"It's cancer, Aston."

"It's what?" I immediately lost my appetite.

"Yeah." slShe nodded slowly.

I shook my head until I got dizzy.

"No. Nah, Ma. No. They gotta be wrong. You're healthy. You just got a cold or something. C'mon, let's go. I'll take you to the doctor right now."

"Baby boy, listen to me. Hear me when I tell you that I've tried it all. I've gotten second, third, and fourth opinions, and they've all told me the same thing. It's cancer, and I'm dying."

I dropped the apple and watched it roll across the floor until it stopped right at her feet. Suddenly, it felt like all the air in the room was being sucked away from my lungs. I couldn't breathe. I sat and stared into my mother's sad eyes. I could see the tears welling up in the corners. I didn't know what to say, and I didn't know how to feel.

"What do you need me to do?" I asked.

Those seven words were all I got out before a tear slipped down my face.

"Don't cry, Aston. Please. You have to be strong for me and your brother."

I shook my head again.

"Why you don't want Law to know?"

"I didn't want to ruin things with his wedding. I just thought it would be too much. Plus, I didn't want that little snake of a girlfriend he was going to marry all in my business."

"I told you that's over now, so why can't I tell him?"

"The time isn't right. I know my son just like I know you. I know what you can handle and when you can handle it, and right now isn't the time."

"I just don't know what I'm supposed to with this shit, Ma."

"You take it, and you move on with it. That's what I'm doing. Just taking it one day at a time."

"I—I just have so many questions. Like, how far along is it? Can they remove it? Are you in any pain? How do you really feel about this shit?"

"It's stage three lung cancer. They said they could operate if I did the chemo and everything, but I'm not doing it."

"What do you mean you're not doing it!" I yelled.

"You heard me. I watched my sister go through it and your grandmother, too. I see what that shit does to people, and I'm not doing it. God gave me this for a reason, so I'm going to live out my final days the way I want to."

I sighed and shook my head. I knew I shouldn't have been mad, but I couldn't help myself. I was pissed off at everything and everybody. I was pissed off at my mother for giving up. I was pissed off that she had cancer in the first place. I was pissed at myself for not coming around as often as I should've. I was pissed at the fucking doctors. I just needed to get out of the house and blow off some steam.

"I gotta go, Ma," I told her as I walked over and kneeled down in front of her.

She pulled me into her fragile arms and kissed my forehead. I looked up at her, and she held both sides of my face.

"We all have our time, baby boy. We can't all be young and healthy forever. I've accepted it, and you will have to, too." She nodded.

I nodded and swallowed the lump that was growing in my throat. I had to get out of there. I climbed to my feet and kissed the palms of my mother's hands.

"I love you," I told her.

"I will always love you more." She nodded.

"I'll call to check up on you soon. I promise."

I turned to walk out of the house and ran back to my car. As soon as I got inside, I punched the steering wheel as hard as I could.

"Fuck!" I yelled as tears of anger and sorrow started leaking out of my eyes.

My mother was the only woman I'd ever said the words "I love you" to. I didn't know how I was going to keep that shit from Law. She was his mother before she became mine, and I just didn't feel like it was right to not tell him, but I also wanted to respect my mother's wishes. I wiped my tears, and my eyes started burning. I reluctantly started the car and listened to the engine purr for a few minutes. I sat there, trying to pull myself together. I heard my phone vibrate against the leather seat. It was Raquel. I sent her call to voicemail and put the phone back down. I figured she was calling me to see why I'd left her at the church. Two seconds went by, and she called me again. I rolled my eyes and picked up.

"Hello?" I answered.

"Blaze! Where are you?"

"I... um... I had some business to handle. What's up?"

"I need you to come get me from the church. Law's been arrested."

* * *

11

Nashiya

Love will make you do some crazy things. You might rob, steal, kill, or in my case, call the fucking police on the nigga who broke my heart. There I was, sitting on Janique's couch on what should've been the happiest day of my life. I let my tears fall onto my $15,000 wedding dress and watched them dissolve into the expensive Italian fabric.

"Here," Janique said, handing me a shot of vodka. "It'll make you feel better."

"To feel better I'd need the entire bottle."

"I got that for you if you need it." She nodded.

"I just don't get it, Nique. I gave him everything!" I sobbed. "I gave him all of me. I gave that nigga more than enough to become his wife!"

"You gave him more than he deserved apparently," she said, patting me on the back.

"All he did was take! This isn't the way my life was supposed to be! I was supposed to be the one sitting next to him on that throne! No other bitch but me! We could've been everything!" I screamed out in pure disgust at how my life was going.

I didn't know if I was more enraged, hurt, embarrassed, or a combination of the three. If I had a daddy, he probably would've warned me about niggas like Law. But knowing me, I probably wouldn't have listened.

"So what are you gonna do?" she asked me as she walked over to her safe and unlocked it.

"What do you mean?" I asked, wiping my tears.

"I mean, the Shiya I know ain't gon' sit around and cry over no nigga. She gon' go out there and get what's hers. So, I'll ask you again—What are you gon' do?"

Janique was right. I was raised to take whatever I wanted whenever I wanted it by any means necessary. I knew that Law had a target on his back. He fucked up letting me in his circle, and I was going to make sure he never lived down what he did to me. If he ever got out of jail, I knew I'd be the first person he'd try to come after, and I was going to be ready. I was going to open Pandora's Box so wide that nobody would be able to close it. Janique walked back over to me and put a pistol on the coffee table. I looked over at her then down at the chrome gun sparkling under the living room light and picked it up.

"I'm going to get what's mine."

CHAPTER TWO

Raquel

"Y**ou know I love you, right, Raquel?"** Law told me as he kissed my forehead.

"I know, and I love you, too."

"Good. And now that Shiya is out of the picture, I don't see any reason as to why we can't be together."

"Are you serious?" I asked, beaming from ear to ear.

"Yeah... so you tryna be mine?"

"Raquel! Raquel! Wake up!" Blaze said, shaking my shoulder. "Huh?"

I slowly adjusted myself in the passenger seat and rubbed my eyes. *It was all a dream,* I thought to myself as I shook my head and tried to focus on what Blaze was talking to me about.

"Wait. Just slow down and start over," I told him.

"Damn, how the fuck can you even sleep at a time like this?"

"I'm sorry. I must have dozed off," I said, shaking my head.

"So tell me what happened again from the beginning, and don't leave shit out."

"We were in the church talking, and then when we opened the doors to walk out, all these fucking cops were there. They told him to put his hands up, and they arrested him right there on the spot for Damien's murder."

"And that's it?" Blaze asked.

"There was this detective there... Detective Mason I think. He said that h—he said that he had the footage of me running out of the hotel the night everything went down," I said, stumbling over my words.

"What the fuck!" Blaze yelled, smacking the steering wheel. "I know it was that mothafucking bitch, Shiya!"

"Yeah. I think it was her, too." I nodded.

"Law ain't gotta worry about shit because I'ma handle that bitch. Believe that." He nodded.

"Blaze, you need to calm down. The last thing we need is for you to be locked up, too."

I sighed and shook my head. It seemed like everybody around me was on pins and needles. I was trying my best to keep a level head, but all I could think about was Law and how he was holding up being in jail. Blaze slowed the car down when his phone rang.

"Hello?" he answered as he turned the music down.

"Yes... Are you sure? Okay, yeah. I'll be there," he said and hung up.

"What? What's going on?"

"Shit, man!"

"Who was that?"

"That was the lawyer. Law's bail has been set at a million fucking dollars."

"Okay, so what's the problem?" I asked.

"That's a lot of money to clean and move at once without looking suspect. I can't show up to jail with a duffel bag full of cash. They'll arrest my ass right on the spot."

"Shit," I mumbled.

The two of us sat in silence, thinking, when Blaze spoke up again.

"I need you to do something for me."

"What?"

"I need you to take some cash I'm about to give you, take the car, and go all over Miami if you have to, and get cashier checks, money orders, whatever you gotta do. Don't get more than five thousand dollars at a time. I'll do the same, and I'll put up ten thousand dollars in cash, but the rest of that shit has to look clean. If we gotta go through a bail bondsman, or whatever, we gon' do it, and just pay that nigga right off. I don't give a fuck what we gotta do. I'm gettin' my brother out of jail tonight."

"Okay, and once we do that, everything will be good?"

"Yeah, Law is coming home. Mark my words, Raquel."

When we pulled up to the house, Blaze ran inside. I walked in and stood inside the foyer. He came back downstairs with a black book bag and handed it to me.

"Here."

"What's in it?" I asked.

"Fucking rainbows and ponies, Raquel. What the fuck do you think is in it? It's cash!"

"Okay, okay."

"Are you sure you can pull this shit off? I know this ain't what you're used to."

"I want him out as bad as you do, Blaze. I can do it," I assured him.

"Okay. Take the keys to the silver BMW and keep that busted ass phone of yours on you. I'll call you when I need you."

I nodded, took the bag and the keys, and left. I ran all over town to 7-Eleven's, check cashing places, banks, and Walmart's until I had $50,000 in clean money. I knew I was far as hell from the million we needed to get Law out of jail, but it was a start.

When I got back in the car, I put the checks and money orders in the bag and realized I had almost two hundred dollars leftover. Instead of running back inside to get another money order, I took the money to plan a special night for Law and I at the penthouse whenever Blaze brought him home. Truth was that my body had been longing for him. I ran into the store and purchased three dozen red roses, tea light candles, strawberries, and a matching lace bra and panty set. If Blaze really was going to get Law out like he promised, I wanted to make sure I welcomed him home in a way that he'd never forget.

* * *

I was flying down Collins Avenue, bobbing and weaving through traffic. I had gotten a few thousand dollars cleaned, but it still wasn't nearly enough to get Law out of the box that I knew they were holding him in. Knowing I had a million thoughts running through my mind all at once, I pulled over into the nearest parking lot and called my mother.

"Baby," she answered.

"Hey, Ma. How you feelin'?"

"I'm okay. I just saw you, remember?"

"Yeah, I know."

"What's wrong?"

I sighed and chewed my bottom lip.

"I'm not tryna stress you, but Law has been arrested, and his bail has been set for a million dollars, and I can't just walk in there with the cash. He'd kill me if I did that."

"Arrested for what?"

"Some shit he didn't do."

"Come back over here. The check will be ready when you get here," she said and hung up.

I put the car in drive and headed back to my mother's house. When I walked in the house twenty minutes later, she was sitting at the kitchen table with a cup of hot tea steaming in front of her.

"I'm here, Ma."

"What happened?" she asked.

"I don't know all the real details, but he got arrested right outside the church. They tryna pin a murder on him."

"Whose murder?"

"That's not important."

"It is if I asked. Do I know him?"

"I don't know. I don't think so. He was one of those Price niggas. You already know it's beef whenever we seem them and vice versa. They killed Wolfe, so he had to go."

"Which one of them was killed, Aston?" she asked in a serious tone.

"Damien, the oldest."

Instead of responding, my mother sat there, stirring her tea around inside the mug. I could tell she was thinking hard about something, but I didn't press her about it.

"Ma, you okay?"

"Bring me my checkbook."

"Are you sure?" I asked.

"How much do you need?" she asked.

"I have it. It's just not clean... at least not all of it." I shrugged.

"Okay, here," she said, handing me a check for one million dollars.

"Ma... I can't," I said, eyeing the check in her hand.

"You say you already have the money, right? But mine is clean. Remember, this is our little secret. It's yours if you don't tell your brother that I'm sick," she said.

I slowly nodded my head. She was always making negotiations, even after she left my father's fast life alone. I looked at her and swallowed hard, knowing I didn't want to know the answer to the question I was about to ask.

"How much longer do you have, Ma?"

"Doctors keep saying if I start an aggressive chemo treatment, then maybe there will be hope, but I keep telling them I'm not doing it."

I shook my head. There was no way.

"I still don't understand why you don't want me to tell Law."

"Clearly, I was right when I told you that your brother has a lot weighing on his shoulders right now. He can't handle this news on top of everything else. I told you I know my kids. I just want him to work on getting out of jail and running the business. That's all."

I sighed and nodded my head. I knew she was right.

"Okay. Now, get out of here and go get your brother out. I love you both," she said as she kissed my forehead again.

"I love you, too, Ma."

I walked out of my mother's house and pulled out my phone to call Clifton. He answered on the second ring.

"Cliff? Yeah, it's me. I got the bail money."

"That's great news. I'll be sure to tell Andreas."

"Yeah, and tell him to hold his head up. I'm just counting down the hours until he comes home, aight? Tell him everything out here good, and he ain't gotta worry about a thing. I got it," I said and hung up.

As soon as I ended the call, I texted Raquel.

Blaze: Everything good. I got the money. Meet me back at the house in 30.

Raquel: Okay.

* * *

Nashiya

I left Janique's house hours later feeling more like myself and not like the sad half of a woman I knew I looked like. When I got back in car to go home, I realized I didn't have a home to go back to. Everything I shared with Law had been snatched away from me in the blink of an eye. I got out of the car and popped the trunk to find my purse. I slipped the gun inside and noticed my license and credit cards were in there. I sighed out of relief and hopped back in my car to head to a hotel until I could figure out what the fuck my next move was going to be.

As soon as I got into my hotel room, I took the wedding dress off and tossed it on the floor like it was a cheap rag. I curled into a ball on the bed with just my white lace bra and panty set and matching garter on. I slowly pulled the large engagement ring off and spun it around my fingertip until my phone rang inside my purse.

I slowly sat up, grabbed my purse from the edge of the bed, and pulled my phone out to look at the screen. It was Dallas.

"What?" I answered.

"What? That's how you answer the phone for a nigga that always comes through for you?" he asked.

I sighed.

"I'm sorry. What's up?"

"I'm surprised you even answered. Weren't you supposed to be Mrs. Calloway by now?"

I scoffed as my nostrils flared. I could feel a new batch of tears starting to form in the corners of my eyes.

"Nah."

That was all I managed to get out before my voice broke up. I put the phone down and put my hand over my mouth. I couldn't let Dallas hear me crying over a nigga I knew he hated. He would never let me live it down.

"Hello? Bird? You there?"

"I'm here," I said, clearing my throat.

I pressed the speaker button and laid back down, trying hard to suppress my tears.

"So what's up? What happened?"

"We didn't get married."

"Damn, for real?"

"Yeah, I called it off."

"What the fuck you go and do that for?"

"I changed my mind about the shit."

"Why do I find that so hard to believe?" he said.

"Nigga, I don't care if you believe it or not. It's what came out of my mouth."

"Yeah, okay. You good though?"

"Nigga, I'm great," I said with an attitude in my tone.

"I'ma just holla at you later when you not feelin' yourself so much."

"Yeah, you do that," I said and hung up.

I tossed the phone across the bed, flipped over, and screamed into the pillow. Talking to Dallas hadn't done anything but piss me the fuck off. Yeah, he'd come through for me when I needed him in more ways than one. He came through for me with trying to get in between Raquel and Law, and he came through for me when he got the copy of the hotel footage from the night things went down and Raquel blew into my life in the first place. He had always been there when I needed him, but my heart still resided with Law. As fucked up as it may have sounded, I still had hope that the two of us would make it through all the bullshit and end up together in the end. I rolled over when I heard my phone ding.

> Dallas: You really know how to piss me the fuck off.

> Shiya: The feeling is mutual...

> Dallas: You gon' stop tryna play me, too. I be tryna be cool and let shit slide, but I'm done with that shit.

I rolled my eyes and put the phone down. Dallas was all bark and no bite when it came to me. All I had to do was give him a little attention every now and then to keep him coming back, and he was good with eating the scraps I fed him right out of my hand. That's exactly how I got him to get the footage from the hotel.

After I met Dallas at Big Pink and looped Raquel's ass into my plan, I doubled back later that night and called him. I knew that once I told him that Raquel was at the hotel the night his brother was killed, he'd want a piece of any action I was going to swing his way.

"*I need you to do something else for me,*" *I said as soon as he picked up the phone.*

"*Damn, two favors in one day. My payout is about to be great,*" *he said.*

"*Shut up and just listen, okay?*"

"*You have all my attention, Bird.*"

"*Okay, so remember what I told you about Raquel being at the hotel the night your brother was killed?*"

"*Yeah, and?*"

"*I can show you proof, but you just gotta get it for me.*"

"*Get it for you? How?*" *he asked.*

"*I need you to go to the hotel and get the security camera footage from that night.*"

"*How the fuck do you think I'm gonna do that?*"

"*You're a resourceful ass nigga. You'll figure it out.*"

"You want me to walk up in there and stick up the place and demand them to hand the fucking tape over? There was a murder there. You already know the police are probably all over that shit. I'm not goin' nowhere near that shit with my dirty hands, Shiya."

I smacked my lips.

"Whatever."

"You can whatever all you want, but you gon' have to find another way. I wanna believe you and shit, but even I got limits."

"Oh, you got limits but you the one who killed Wolfe, remember that?"

"Are you fucking tryna blackmail me right now, Bird? Because I'm not the nigga you wanna do that with," Dallas growled into the receiver.

"All I'm sayin' is I know your secrets, nigga. All I want you to do is this one thing for me. Nothing else."

"You said that shit the last time, right? Ain't that what got that nigga, Wolfe pushin' up flowers in the first place? You tryna come at me like you know my secrets, but I know yours, too."

I hung up on Dallas and tossed the phone across the room. I was going to have to figure out how to get the footage myself. The next morning, I got up early and planned to drop by the hotel before Raquel and I went to eat, but Dallas texted me and told me he'd gotten the copy. I walked downstairs and stepped into Law's office to call Dallas.

"Hello?" he answered.

"So you really got it?" I asked.

"Yeah. It was actually easier than I thought it would be."

"How'd you do it?"

"I walked in there and asked for a copy of the tape."

"And that's it? They handed it over to you just like that?"

"Nah. Not at first, but all I had to do was flash a little wad of money past the nigga who was workin' behind the counter, and he made it happen. You know they asses only make a couple hundred every two weeks anyway."

"So when can I get it?"

"When do you want it?" he asked.

I playfully bit my lip although I knew he couldn't see me.

"I'll text you later when I can meet you," I said and hung up.

Once Dallas strolled into the restaurant where Raquel and I were sitting, I could tell he was about to start something good. She was in awe, hanging on his every word while trying to play it cool. A part of me got a little jealous, but I made sure to keep a straight face. When Dallas went to write his number down on a napkin for her, she was so wrapped up in getting his ten digits, that she didn't even see him drop the flash drive into my purse underneath the table. He made sure to keep her focus on his lips and not his hands when he said something slick to her right before he left to keep her wanting more.

At first, I intended to keep the flash drive for safe keeping just in case that bitch, Raquel, ever tried something, but the moment Law told me that he wasn't ever going to make me his wife, everything changed. I decided right then and there to take the flash drive straight to the police. If he wanted to break my heart, I was going to make sure his ass never saw the light of day again. It was evident that my heart was broken, but my pride was damaged beyond repair. I had never been that embarrassed in my life.

I ran out of the church, got into the limo, and told the driver to take me to the nearest precinct. When he pulled up, I got out, wiped the smeared mascara stains off my face, and walked through the doors. I put the flash drive in the hands of the nearest police officer and told his ass that once he watched the tape, he'd know who killed Damien Price, but just in case he had a hard time figuring it out, his name was Andreas Calloway.

"But the streets call him Law..."

Ian

I was plotting in my holding cell when a guard came to get me.

"Calloway, come with me."

"What's going on?" I asked.

"Your bail has been posted. You're being released," he told me.

Although I'd only been in lock up for a few hours, I never thought I'd see the day where I'd be fighting for my freedom, especially for a trigger I didn't pull, but it was what it was. Once I went through the process of getting my shit back, the guard walked me out to the front. I looked up and saw Blaze standing there. He smiled when he saw my face. The guard unlocked the handcuffs from around my wrists, and I walked over to hug my brother.

"How are you feelin'? You good?" he asked.

"Yeah. I'm straight."

"You only been in this bitch for what? Like six hours? And you already look big as fuck," he joked.

"Nah, your ass just don't pay attention to what I really look like. That's all." I chuckled.

Blaze and I walked out to the car and got in.

"So what's the lawyer saying?" he asked as he pulled off.

"Clifton said that the D.A.'s evidence is bullshit. They don't have my car anywhere near the scene. They don't have my fingerprints on shit or nothing. I'm not trippin'."

"So what do they have?"

"They have the video footage of Raquel running out of the fucking hotel with blood on her, no shoes, and shit. I thought I told you to handle it, Blaze. If you were going to handle Damien's ass, you should've made sure you tied up all the loose ends!"

"I thought Raquel was the loose end," he said, shaking his head. "My bad. I fucked up. I can fix it, though. Just give me some time."

"No, you can't. I don't want you anywhere near this shit. There's a detective sniffin' around, and I don't know what the fuck his problem is, but he wants me bad. If you get too close, he could find out what really happened that night, and I'm not having that shit."

"Yeah, but I did the shit. I would never let you do my time for me, Law."

"If it came down to that, you wouldn't have a choice. I am my brother's keeper. You already know that."

"I just want you to know I'm in this shit with you every step of the way. When you feel pain, I feel that shit, too. I owe you everything, nigga. Hear me when I say that."

"It's love. Always, baby. Forever." I nodded.

"But for real though, Law. Thank you, man."

"For what?"

"You know for what. For always holding me down no matter what. All this court shit and the lawyers and charges and shit... I don't feel right lettin' you do all this."

"You ain't gotta worry about shit, Blaze. I already told you. I'm my brother's keeper. Ain't shit changed."

"I know, but..."

"But nothing, Cliff is handling it. We gon' be straight. No matter if you wrong or right, I'll lay a nigga down for you. I'll do time for you because you my blood. All we got is us," I assured him.

"I just don't know how the fuck they got the tape anyway," Blaze said, sounding confused.

"I do."

"How?"

"Shiya. I already know she's the mastermind behind this whole shit," I said, shaking my head.

"Damn, yo. That bitch did you dirty like that? And that fucking fast?"

"I know. Shit is crazy."

"Question is... what are you going to do about it?"

"I'm going to let her dig her own grave for now. But don't worry... She gon' pay."

"She probably dealin' with those Price niggas, huh? Out of respect for you, that's the only reason any of them mothafuckas is still breathing. I swear. They don't want no problems."

"Enough about that bitch and them niggas. They gon' feel it sooner than later. How's Raquel?" I asked.

"She's good. I can tell she misses you."

"I miss her, too. Shit is just crazy right now. Is she back at the house yet?"

"Nah. She still at the penthouse."

"Okay. Bet." I nodded. "Take me to the crib. I'm gonna take a shower and shit, and then I'm gonna go see what's up with her."

"Say no more."

Before Shiya, nobody had ever played me for no sucker ass nigga. I'd made a million dollars millions of times, but I'd never had my heart broken once. I didn't even know if it was broken. I didn't feel hurt. She crossed me, and all it did was leave me scarred and angry as hell. My heart could've been bleeding and I couldn't feel it. All I wanted to do was see Raquel, keep my eyes open for snakes, get back at anybody who fucked with me, and pray that the Feds never came and got me again.

Blaze pulled up to the house, and I hopped out of the car. It felt so good to be home. As soon as I got in my room, I plugged my phone up to the charger and went into the bathroom to turn on the shower. Once I got myself together, I got dressed, grabbed my phone, keys, wallet, and headed out to my car. I sat behind the wheel and checked my phone for the first time in hours. I had a few missed calls from Alastair. I figured word had somehow gotten back to him about my arrest, so I called him back.

"That must be one hell of a lawyer you've got," he answered.

"Yeah, something like that."

"I'm glad you're out."

"I'm glad to be out." I nodded.

"We need to meet ... to talk. It's not safe to talk on the phone. Meet me tomorrow at the Catalina Hotel in South Beach on the rooftop pool at dusk."

"Okay." I nodded and hung up.

I pressed the button to start my car and sped off my property with one thing on my mind—seeing Raquel. When I got to the penthouse, I knocked on the door and took a step back. A few seconds later, Raquel opened it wearing a matching red lace bra and panty set, black heels, and a smile.

"Hi." She smiled.

"Hello to you, too," I smiled back.

"You weren't expecting another nigga were you?" I asked.

"Nobody but you, Law. Come in."

Raquel grabbed my hand and led me into the dimly lit penthouse. There were hundreds of rose petals scattered everywhere and candles, too.

"I've never planned anything romantic before, so I hope this is okay," she told me.

"I've never had anybody plan anything romantic for me before, so this is perfect, Raquel."

"Great," she said as she walked into the kitchen and rested her elbows on the countertop.

"You look beautiful by the way."

"You don't look so bad yourself." She smiled.

"How'd you know I'd come?"

"Blaze told me you were getting out, so... I just figured you'd want to see me as much as I wanted to see you." She shrugged.

"Well, you were right about that. Did you miss me?"

"You can't tell?" she asked as she looked around the room.

I smiled and nodded.

"You right. Come here then. Why you standing over there actin' scared of a nigga?"

Raquel walked over to me, and I wrapped my arms around her small waist. She softly pecked my lips, leaving a little residue of her cotton candy lip gloss on me. I licked my lips.

"Mmm. You taste good and you smell good, too."

I drew her in close to me and nuzzled my head in the crevice between her left shoulder and neck then gently kissed her collarbone.

"Today was crazy, right?" she asked as she backed away from me.

"I don't want to talk about today."

"What do you want to talk about then?"

"You and me," I told her.

"What about us?"

"I want to see what else you had up your sleeve. It's real sexy in here right now. A nigga is feelin' it." I laughed.

"Well, I've got some strawberries, whipped cream, handcuffs ..."

"Nah, I'm good on those." I chuckled as I shook my head.

"Oh shit. Sorry." She blushed.

I couldn't stop shaking my head at her. I couldn't take my eyes off her either. She was simply beautiful. I felt good knowing that she had went out of her way to make my homecoming special. Just looking at the way she was standing in those heels made my dick throb.

"Stop runnin' away from me, Raquel, and come here. I missed you."

I walked over to Raquel and pinned her against the countertop so she couldn't run. I looked down and kissed her soft lips gently and let my hands roam all over her body. I slid my finger inside her panties and felt the heat radiating off her tight ass pussy. I smiled. Nothing felt better than knowing her pussy was all mine. I lifted Raquel up and sat her on the edge of the countertop then dropped down to slide off her heels one by one. I massaged her feet and then started sucking her toes. Her legs trembled.

"Mmm... Did you miss daddy, Raquel?"

"Mmmhm..." She nodded.

"You gon' show me how much?" I asked.

"Yes."

Raquel slid her foot out of my hands and hopped off the countertop. She grabbed my hand and led me back into the bedroom where there were more rose petals scattered all over the bed and the floor.

"Damn, you really went all out," I told her.

She climbed on the bed and twerked for me a little. I reached out to massage her ass and smack it. She looked back at me and smiled.

"Do you like what you see?"

"You really must have missed me." I grinned.

"I did." She nodded.

I reached out and massaged her breasts that looked like they were about to jump straight out of her bra. Raquel scooted over to the edge of the bed and started unbuckling my jeans. I stood and watched her as she started to unzip my pants. She pulled my pants down and watched them fall around my ankles and then slid my hardening dick out through the slit in my boxer briefs.

"Tell me how you like it," she said as she slowly slipped my dick into her mouth.

"Mmm, shit," I groaned. "Just like that."

Raquel slid my dick out of her mouth and got up to grab the bottle of champagne sitting on ice on the nightstand. I stepped out of my pants and my boxers and stood there as she dropped to her knees, took the bottle of champagne, and poured some on my dick then proceeded to slurp and lick it off.

"Damn," I said as I gently cuffed the back of her neck.

She bobbed up and down on my dick with her mouth and then took my dick into her hand to jack me off as she sucked on the head. I latched my hand underneath her chin and drove her warm mouth onto my dick.

"Mmm... shit, Raquel," I said as I placed my right hand under her chin and the other on top of her head.

She massaged my balls and sucked my dick for a few more minutes until I stopped her. I was ready to lay the pipe.

"Stand up, baby."

Raquel stood to her feet, and I laid her on the bed, pulling her to the edge of it and spreading her legs. I licked my fingers and rubbed them down her clit and then slid my dick inside her. As soon as the head pushed through, her pussy grabbed a tight hold of it.

"Goddamn," I groaned.

I held her right leg in the air as I thrusted into her with slow, long strokes.

"Mmm... shit," she moaned.

"You like that shit, Raquel?"

"I love that shit, baby."

"You gon' come ride daddy's dick?"

"Mmhm..." she whimpered.

"Come ride daddy's dick then," I told her.

I laid on my back and she climbed on top of me. I wrapped my hands around her waist and slowly lowered her down onto my dick. Raquel started riding my dick slow at first, trying to catch the rhythm. I let her bounce up and down on my dick until she was comfortable. Then I grabbed her by her ass and thrust upward into her.

"Ooohhhh... shit," she moaned, sucking in air through her teeth.

Raquel could barely breathe as she screamed out in pleasure. I slammed her ass down on my dick and fucked her faster. I could feel myself nearing my nut, so I switched positions. I started fucking her from the side and watched her titties jiggle with every stroke. Her eyes were slammed shut, and she was biting on her bottom lip so hard I just knew she was going to draw blood.

"Yeah, that's it. Keep biting that lip, baby," I groaned.

"Mmmm..." she moaned.

She reached back and rubbed my chest, clawing at it with her nails as her moans got louder.

"Turn around and let me hit that pussy from the back."

Raquel got on all fours and arched her back a little. Her back and ass were glistening with sweat. I pumped into her and watched her ass jiggle back against my dick. I pushed her back down so she could arch her ass up higher in the air. I pulled my dick out and slapped it against her ass cheeks then slid back inside her.

"Back that pussy up on this dick, Raquel," I demanded as I smacked her ass.

"Ooohhhh shiiiittt, Law!" she screamed.

"You like that shit?"

"Yes, baby, I do!"

"Mmm... Turn over and let me see your face, baby," I told her.

I pulled out of her, and she rolled over onto her back. I rubbed my hard, wet dick against her juicy pussy then slowly slid back inside her. I reached up and grabbed her breast and gave her nipple a squeeze.

"Mmm... shit," I groaned, as I pumped in and out of her while slowly grinding my hips.

"Mmm. Right there."

"Right there, Raquel?"

"Mmm. Yes, Law. Right there!"

She was panting as she looked down at my dick and watched it slowly slide in and out of her.

"Your pussy feels so good."

"Your dick feels good, too, baby."

I could see her pussy glistening as she creamed. I licked my lips.

"Oh my God!" She trembled, as she climaxed.

I fucked her faster so she could ride out the wave of her orgasm and then came inside her.

"Fuckkkkk," I groaned.

I collapsed onto her body as we both tried to catch our breath. I slowly slid out of her and repositioned myself to lay beside her.

"You know you comin' home with me, right?" I smiled.

CHAPTER THREE
Raquel

L
aw and I laid in bed together, holding hands. He was the perfect mix of a gentleman and a gangster in my eyes. I loved every bit of him from the top of his head to the soles of his feet. I was happy to know that he missed me just as much as I'd missed him, even if it hadn't been a whole twenty-four hours.

"I should get up," I told him.

"What's the rush?" he asked.

"No rush," I said. "I just know you're supposed to go to the bathroom before and after sex."

"You always play by the rules, huh?"

"Not when it comes to you." I smiled. "I'll be right back."

I went to the bathroom, freshened up and came back out.

"Hey, I was thinking ..."

"What is this, Raquel?" he asked, holding Detective Mason's card in his hand as he sat on the edge of the bed.

I sighed.

"It's not what it looks like. I was approached by a detective outside of the church when you were arrested."

"And what? Why the fuck am I just now hearing about this?"

"For one, your ass was in jail, and two, because there was nothing for you to hear, Law!"

"What did he say?" he asked.

"He just said that if they could pin you for the murder of Damien, then they could put you away for good."

"And what did you say to that?"

"I told him I didn't know anything."

"Did you make it believable? Huh? Did you?" he asked, balling up the business card in his hand.

"Yes! Of course, I did! What kind of question is that? I don't even know why you're so mad at me right now! I could've gotten a get out of jail free card, but I didn't! I stuck with you!"

"What the fuck are you talking about?" he asked.

"Law... he said they've got me on tape running from the hotel that night."

Law sighed and shook his head.

"Did he tell you how they got it?"

"No! I don't know! He said that he had a copy of the tape and the recording of the call I made to 911," I sighed.

Law shook his head and lowered his voice.

"Are you sure you didn't tell him anything, Raquel? Does he want you to testify?"

"I don't know. He hasn't said anything to me since we were at the church."

"Man, fuck!" he yelled.

"Law, you just got out of jail. I need you to calm down."

"Calm down? Raquel, one fuck up and this mothafucka is going to try and lock me up for some shit I didn't even do. We're talking first degree murder and a minimum of twenty years if I take the plea deal."

Law got up and started redressing, mumbling to himself.

"Law... look at me."

"What?" he said as he turned to face me.

"I know you didn't do it, but if you didn't, then who really killed Damien?"

"The police are watching you, Raquel. Do you really think I'd tell you? It's called plausible deniability," he told me as he put his shirt on.

I sighed and then nodded slowly. He was right. The less I knew, the better off I'd be in the long run.

"I don't trust his ass!"

"Who?" I asked.

"That fucking detective."

"Yeah, I don't like him either."

"Don't worry about it. I'll handle it."

"Do you think Shiya had anything to do with it?"

"I don't think; I know. She was the only other person that could've went to the police about the shit that she knew."

"Why though? All because you called off the wedding?"

Law shrugged.

"I don't know... Maybe. But I don't want you to worry about none of this court shit, the Shiya shit, none of it. I'm gonna handle it all."

"You keep saying that, but you're not telling me *how* you're going to 'handle' these things," I said, emphasizing the word handle with air quotes.

"Look, Raquel, I don't know how deep all this Shiya shit goes, but that bitch is dead to me. I was just a pawn to that bitch, and I'm gon' take care of her. That's all you need to know."

I sighed and nodded.

"Okay."

"Look, at the end of the day, the shit I'm facing is real, aight? This ain't no going off to war shit, Raquel. If they take me down for this, I'm done. I may as well be dead. I need to know that I can really trust you and that you're serious about holding me down."

"Law, you know how I feel about you, and even if you don't love me, I ..."

"Shh," he said as he placed he finger over my lips and kissed me.

I grabbed his hand as he rested it on my cheek then kissed it. With all the feelings I had inside me for Law, it killed me that he couldn't reciprocate them back. Sometimes I felt like I was in love all by myself, but I still couldn't leave him alone. I knew he probably needed me more in that moment than he probably ever would, and I was going to stay true to my word and stick by his side.

* * *

Law

"C'mon and put some real clothes on, and let's head back to the house," I told her.

Raquel nodded slowly and threw on a pair of sweatpants and a tank top. When she first started staying with me, she had nothing but the bloodstained dress she came in with. Once I realized I just couldn't get rid of her, I had Blaze go out and buy her some clothes and other necessities. She still didn't have a full wardrobe, but I was going to change that. I could tell by the look on her face and her body language that something was bothering her. She wasn't a hard person to read. She'd been wearing her heart on her sleeve from the moment I met her, and nothing had changed about that.

All she wanted was a nigga to tell her I loved her, but I knew better. I could've probably given Raquel the world, but I couldn't tell her I loved her, even if I did. Truth was, I didn't know where the chips were going to fall with my situation, and I just wasn't ready for another let down when it came to a female.

"I'm ready to go," she said.

Raquel and I left the penthouse and went back to my house. She didn't say much of anything to me the entire ride there.

"You okay?" I asked as I pulled in front of the house and shut off the engine.

"Mmhm... I'm fine."

"You sure?"

"Yeah," she said as she got out of the car.

She started walking toward the door and stopped to wait for me to unlock it. When I opened it, she went straight upstairs into her old room and closed the door behind her. I sighed and walked up the stairs and knocked on her door. Instead of waiting for her to open it, I opened it myself.

"For real, Raquel? What's your problem? You been actin' funny since we left the penthouse."

"I can't explain it." She shrugged.

"Try."

"I don't know. I thought I'd be happy to be here with you, but this isn't my house. This is the house you shared with another female. A female that you were going to marry. I'm just uncomfortable, and I'm not going anywhere near your room."

I tried to stop myself from laughing and nodded instead.

"Understandable. I'll sleep in here with you if you want me to, and I'll make sure all of Shiya's things are placed in bags and thrown out. To make everything better, I'll replace her things with a whole new wardrobe for you."

I saw a smile creep up on her face as she looked at me.

"Really?"

"Yeah, really." I nodded.

"Thank you."

"You deserve it. You're perfect."

"Stop saying that, baby. I'm not perfect."

"Well, you're perfect for me, so that's all that matters. But um... are you good for a little bit? I'm going to go holla at Blaze and then I'll come back. Cool?"

"Yeah. Do your thing. I'll be fine," she told me.

I pulled Raquel into my chest and kissed her forehead, then turned to leave the room. I went downstairs to my office where Blaze was sitting and closed the door.

"So what's up? What did you want to talk to me about?" Blaze asked as he yawned.

"That fucking detective."

"What about him?"

"He talked to Raquel. I found his card in her room."

"So what are you thinking?" he asked.

"I don't know yet." I shrugged.

"You think she had something to do with it?"

"No. Hell no. I just don't know how she's gonna handle it if he comes back around and starts applying pressure. She ain't never been in no situation like this before."

"I can handle him if you want me to."

I quickly shook my head in his direction.

"We are not killing a fucking cop. Your *handling* shit is how we got in this mess in the first place."

"So tell me what you wanna do. I'll follow your lead with this, Law. I won't pull no more triggers unless you ask me to," Blaze said.

"Right now, I've got a target on my back. Between Shiya, those Price niggas, and that fucking detective, I don't know who is gonna try to strike first, or when."

"Man, fuck them niggas and that bitch, too. I might not be able to kill a cop, but I can damn sure make sure nobody ever sees the three of them again."

"Nah, I got it. We have to go meet Al at dusk tomorrow down in South Beach."

"Aight, bet. I'ma head to bed. I'll holla at you in the morning."

"Night," I told him.

I pulled out my phone and looked at the time. It was almost 4:00 a.m. Blaze closed the door behind him, and I took a seat behind the desk. I reached into my desk drawer and pulled out a blunt and my lighter. Although I was glad to be home, I felt like I hadn't slept in weeks. My paranoia was at an all-time high. I felt like I was trying to survive in the wildest jungle, and all I had to use as a weapon was my mind.

Smoke flew threw my nostrils as I exhaled, trying to release my thoughts and anxiety all at the same time. I had a heavy heart over my situation. I didn't want to go to jail, but if I was going to go, I was going to make sure I wreaked havoc on a lot of mothafuckas before they locked my ass up and threw away the key.

I took one last pull from the blunt and got up to walk over and check my safe. I always kept a couple hundred thousand tucked away for a rainy day. I flipped through the wads of money and then reached in the back to grab my father's gun. He'd given it to Wolfe, and when Wolfe died, I took ownership of it. I walked over and put it in my top drawer and closed it then went upstairs to lay next to Raquel.

When I got to the room, she was already in the bed with the lights off, fast asleep. I pulled my shirt over my head and stepped out of my shoes, socks, and jeans then crawled in bed beside her. It felt good to be lying next to her. At the end of the day, all I wanted to do was protect her, my family, and continue to hold my own.

* * *

The Next Night...

Blaze and I went to the Catalina Hotel in South Beach to meet Alastair. When we stepped off the elevator to the rooftop pool, Alastair was sitting in the back cabana with a drink in one hand and a Cuban cigar in the other.

"Join me," he told us as he blew smoke out of his nostrils.

Blaze and I walked over and sat with him as he sipped his dark-colored drink. He offered us both a drink, but we refused.

"So what did you want to meet for?" I asked.

Alastair sighed, looked me in the eye, and then took another sip of his drink.

"You need to lay low. Shit is hot right now," he said.

"I already know that." I nodded.

"I'll provide you one last shipment, but then I'm going back to Texas for a while."

"Hold up. You're leaving?" Blaze asked.

"Yeah. Miami is not a good look for me right now. Once shit dies down with your case, I'll make my way back, but for now, I think it's gonna be better for business if I move on."

Before Blaze could say anything else, I cut him off.

"When do you leave?" I asked Alastair.

"In a few days. I'll make sure everything goes good with your shipment first, and then I'm out."

"Are you doing the same for the Prices?" Blaze asked.

"You should know enough about me by now to know that I don't discuss business that don't concern you. I'll be in touch when your shipment drops."

"Respect." I nodded.

I got up, and Blaze followed suit. We didn't say anything to each other until we got in the car outside.

"I think that mothafucka is playing us," Blaze said as he fastened his seat belt.

"Me too." I nodded.

"So, what we gon' do about it?"

"Don't worry about it. I got a plan."

Even though shit was fucked up, I still had love for the game because it was all about moves and countermoves. It was time for Blaze and I to level the fuck up. If Alastair was leaving, that meant that once we got our shipment, the Prices would probably be getting their last as well. That's when I knew what I was going to do. I was going to hit them where I knew it would hurt them the most—their pockets.

CHAPTER FOUR
Raquel

I was sitting in the house, flipping through channels when my phone rang. I looked down at the cracked screen and almost didn't want to even answer it. I hated that phone simply because Shiya had given it to me. For all I knew, her snake ass was tracking all my phone calls. I let the call go to voicemail and then my phone rang again. The number had a South Carolina area code. I sighed and picked it up.

"Hello?"

"Raquel? Is that you?" the caller asked.

"Who is this?"

"So you don't know my voice now?"

"Derrick?" I asked.

"Yeah, it's me," he said.

My heart nearly sunk down to my feet. I hadn't heard his voice or heard from him since I caught him fucking my roommate on the night of my graduation.

"Wow ..."

"How are you?" he asked.

"How'd you get this number?"

"Camille gave it to me."

"Wow..." I scoffed, ready to go off on her.

"Please don't hang up!" he begged.

"What do you want?"

"I just want to talk to you. I... When you didn't come back

from Miami with Camille and Shante, I didn't know what to think. I knew you were mad at me and weren't answering my calls, but then when I ran into Camille and she told me that she hadn't heard from you, I got really worried."

"What? Did you think I killed myself over you or something?" I asked with attitude running all through my tone.

"No, nothing like that. I just... I don't know. I freaked out. I damn near went to the police over you."

"You didn't do that, did you?" I asked as my eyes widened.

"No, I didn't. I knew in my heart that you were okay. I'm just so happy to hear your voice after all this time. It's been months, Raqi," he said.

"Don't call me that."

"I'm sorry... How have you been?" he asked.

"Fine," I said dryly.

"Camille said you got a job out in Miami."

"Yup."

"Doing what?"

"Where is this really going, Derrick? I don't have time for your bullshit."

He blew air out of his nose and into the receiver.

"I just wanted to apologize to you, okay? I want to apologize for everything. I'd been calling your old number for over a month. I figured you were mad, but then when I ran into Camille this last time, she told me you had a new number. I practically twisted her arm for it."

"Okay, so ..."

"I'll be in Miami in about a week."

"For what?"

"Work."

"Since when does your job let you travel?"

"I got a new job. You know I was interning at that law firm before I graduated, and then I ended up getting hired as a paralegal."

"Oh," was all I got past my lips.

"Yeah, so I'm coming down for a company retreat."

"Mmhm." I nodded.

"So can I see you?" he asked.

"I don't think that's a good idea."

"Why not?"

"What would be the point? I don't have anything to say to you. I don't even know why I'm still on the phone with you at this point."

"Can you just promise me you'll think about it? Maybe when I'm actually there, you'll change your mind? All I'm asking for is a lunch or dinner with you to talk. That's all," he said.

"I'll think about it," I told him.

"Okay, thanks. I'll hit you up in about a week. Take care, Raquel."

"Bye, Derrick," I said, and hung up.

I huffed as I tossed the phone beside me on the bed. I couldn't believe Camille had went against girl code and gave Derrick my number. I also couldn't believe that he and I would be in the same city for the first time in months. I picked up my phone again to call Camille. I hadn't spoken to her since the last time I'd reached out to call her from my new phone. Although we ended the call on good terms, I had a new bone to pick with her.

Truth was, my relationship with Camille was different than most. I was a loner, and so was she. We could go weeks or even months without speaking and pick right up where we left off like nothing ever happened. That's just the type of relationship we had. I sat and waited for Camille to pick up.

"Hello?" she answered.

"Camille!"

"Hey, girl."

"Hey, girl? That's all you're going to say to me?" I asked with a hint of attitude yet again.

"Uh... What exactly did you want me to say?" she asked.

"Um... How about, 'Hey, Raquel. I'm sorry for giving your ex-fiancé your phone number!'"

Camille sighed into the phone.

"Shit, I didn't think his pressed ass was really going to have the balls to call you! I thought he was gonna shoot you a text or something at the most."

"Bitch, he called me twice!"

"Twice? Damnnnn! My bad, girl."

"Yeah, your bad," I said, shaking my head.

"I'm not that sorry though, because I knew if he did contact you, that would be the only way you would call me. Two months is a long time to go without speaking to one another, even for you. What's really going on?"

"What do you mean? I told you everything."

"Yeah. You gave me some bullshit line about how you've got a new man and a new job, but that's not like you, Raquel. I'm not feeling this new version of you." She huffed.

"New version of me? Really?"

"Yeah. That's exactly what I said."

"Why can't you just be happy for me?" I asked.

"It's not that I'm not happy. It's just I don't know what there is for me to be happy about."

"Aren't you the one who told me that the best way to get over a man is to get underneath a new one? Huh? Weren't those your words?"

"Yeah. You're right. I did say that, but since when did your goodie two shoes ass start listening to me anyway? Huh?"

"I guess since now." I shrugged.

"I guess since like two months ago," she said, throwing my attitude right back at me.

I huffed and took the phone away from my ear as I tried to remain cool.

"Look, Camille, there are just some things going on right now that you just wouldn't understand."

"Try me," she said.

"I can't."

"Why not, Raquel?"

45

"Just know that I can't, okay? I just want you to be the same friend you've always been to me, and trust me in all of this."

"You're making that very hard for me, Raqi. Very, very hard." She sighed.

"I'm sorry... Just know if I could, I would. You *know* I would."

"Is there anything you can tell me?" she asked.

I paused for a second and then spoke up.

"His name is Andreas, and I love him," I told her.

"Wow ..."

"Yeah." I nodded.

"And that's it? That's all you're going to give me?"

"Yes... for now."

Camille sighed into the receiver, and I knew she was probably rolling her eyes a thousand times at me. I was grateful that we were having the conversation over the phone and not face to face.

"So..."

"So what?" I asked.

"So, what did Derrick want?"

"To see me. He said he'll be down in Miami in a week or something."

"Oh shit. So, are you going to meet with his ass?"

"I don't know." I shrugged.

"What do you mean you don't know?"

"I just don't know! I told him I'd think about it. Truth be told, I haven't really thought about Derrick that much since I've been gone."

"Sounds like you haven't thought about much else but that nigga you been laid up under since you've been gone. No shade. I'm just stating the facts."

"What do you want me to say, Camille? That I'm sorry for going ghost the way I did? Because if that's what you want, then okay. Yeah, I'm sorry. My bad!"

"Raquel, I've known you for a long ass time, and I know the type of person you are, so excuse me if I'm just a little thrown off by the moves you've been making lately. That's all. I'm not knocking you for it. I'm just saying you could've handled things differently. Shante and I were damn near ready to file a missing person's report on you!"

"Derrick said the same thing," I said, shaking my head.

"We were worried, but then I told myself Raquel and I don't speak every day, and we damn sure don't see each other every day, so she's probably okay. That's the only thing that calmed me down."

"I'm glad you know me." I smiled.

"Still don't make the shit right though."

"For the last time, Camille, I'm sorry, okay? Lemme spell it out for you. I'm S—O—R—R—Y!"

Camille laughed and so did I.

"So, hold up. If you so-call love this new nigga. What's his name again?"

"Andreas," I told her.

"Yeah, him. So, if you so-call love Andreas, then did you uh... you know... let him tap that?"

I didn't say anything. Instead, I let the silence answer for me.

"Oh my God! Bitch! You did it, didn't you!" she yelled into the receiver.

I quickly pulled the phone away from my ear before she ruptured my eardrum.

"Yes, I did. Calm down!"

"How can I calm down after hearing news like that? My bitch done finally let a nigga pop that pussy! Aww, shit, Raquel is poppin' that pussy for a real nigga! I don't believe it! I'm in shock! Like, you should see me right now. I'm holding my chest like Fred Sanford!" she joked.

I laughed and shook my head.

"You're a trip. You know that?"

"So... fill me in. Give me the details. How was it?"

"It was... the most painful pleasure I've ever experienced," I told her.

"Damn, Raquel. That was a beautiful ass description, bitch."

"It was, huh?" I chuckled.

"Hell yeah. I can't wait to meet this nigga. Are you ever going to make that happen? Didn't you tell me you might be coming home soon the last time we talked? What's up with that? Is that still in the works? Have your flights been booked? I mean, what's up?"

"No, not yet."

Camille sighed.

"You're really killing me, bitch. Like, really. I can't! I'm going to be thirty-seven and married with kids by the time I see your ass again!"

"Stop being extra. You know it won't be that long."

"Yeah, okay," Camille said.

"Stop."

"Stop what?"

"Rolling your eyes. I can't even see you, and I know that's what you're doing right now."

Camille burst out laughing and then smacked her lips together.

"Shut up!"

"But are we good, though?" I asked.

"Yeah. We always good. Just stop disappearing, okay?"

"Deal." I nodded.

"Okay then. I'll talk to you later."

"Okay. I love you," I told her.

"Love you, too."

I hung up the phone and fell back against the bed. There were so many thoughts racing through my head from Law to Derrick and Camille. If I did decide to meet up with Derrick, I didn't know how Law would take it if he found out or if I told him beforehand. I honestly didn't even know if I was ready to face him after all that had happened between us. I was so focused on being hurt and angry that I never really dealt with my feelings for him, whether positive or negative. I sighed and put my phone on the nightstand, rolled over, and fell asleep hugging my pillow.

* * *

The Next Day...

I was out browsing the department stores in the mall. I figured a little retail therapy would do me some good, even if I wasn't going to actually purchase anything. I was walking around the store, picking up things, and putting them back again when someone tapped me on the shoulder. I turned to see Detective Mason standing behind me.

"Hello, Miss Valentine. Can I have a word with you?" he asked.

"How long have you been standing there?" I asked, feeling uncomfortable.

"Not long."

I shook my head. I could see why Law was so paranoid all the time. I never even noticed I was being followed.

"What do you want?" I asked as I put a shirt back on the rack.

"All I'm asking you to do, Raquel, is testify."

"Testify? About what?" I asked.

"What you saw that night at the hotel. The night Damien Price was murdered in cold blood."

"I already told you I don't know anything, and I didn't see anything."

"You know why I find that hard to believe?"

"Why?" I asked as I folded my arms across my chest.

"Your story doesn't match up to the video of you running out of the hotel with blood on you or the 911 call you made to the dispatcher."

I sighed loudly.

"What do you want from me?" I asked.

"All I want is the truth, Raquel. I don't want you. I want Andreas."

"You want to know the truth? The truth is you're getting on my nerves, and I'm pretty sure that you following me is harassment, and I'm about ready to file a complaint. You're profiling me. You say you don't want me, but you're tailing me like I'm a suspect or a criminal or something."

"I apologize if I made you feel that way."

"Yeah. It's unacceptable. I'm extremely uncomfortable, and I would appreciate it if you left me the hell alone from here on out!" I said as I walked around the rack and picked up another shirt.

"I don't know what type of mind games Andreas is playing with you or what you think all of this is, but you can make this easy or you can make it hard. Just know I'm down to play hardball, *Miss* Valentine. Enjoy the rest of your shopping."

Detective Mason turned to leave me standing in the midst of racks of clothing and walked out of the store. I slammed the shirt I had in my hand back on the rack and stormed out of the store to go home and warn Law about the unwanted encounter I had.

When I got in the house, I walked through yelling Law's name until I heard him in the bathroom. He was washing his hands.

"What's wrong?" he asked me as he stood in the doorway.

"It's that fucking detective! He won't leave me the fuck alone!"

"What happened?"

"I was in the mall, minding my fucking business in the store, when he just rolls up on me, taps me on my shoulder, and basically asks me to fucking testify against you about what I saw that night at the hotel!"

He sighed and shook his head.

"And when was this?"

"Just now! Like twenty fucking minutes ago! I told his ass that I was going to file a complaint if he didn't stop following me around like I was the fucking criminal!"

"What did he say to that?"

"He said that he didn't want me and all he wanted was you.

He said that you were running mind games on me, and he was down to play hardball if that's what it came down to."

"What the fuck is this mothafucka even talking about?"

"I don't know," I said, shaking my head. "All I know is I'm fucking done with his ass and all his requests!"

"Okay. Don't worry about it. Just calm down."

"No! I can't calm down, Law! This shit is ridiculous, and none of this would ever be happening if it wasn't for that fucking bitch, Nashiya! Oooh, I swear to God that girl needs to get what's coming to her!" I fumed.

Law looked at me and started smiling.

"What are you smiling at?" I asked him.

"You."

"What the hell is so funny?"

"Nothing. I've just never seen you mad before. You look good as shit. I like it," he told me.

I rolled my eyes and then flashed him a half smile. Law pulled me into his arms and kissed my forehead.

"I'm gonna take care of it, okay? All of it."

"Okay." I nodded.

* * *

Law

Once I calmed Raquel down, I pulled out my phone and called Blaze.

"What's up?" he answered.

"Yo, where you at?" I asked.

"Almost to the crib. What's up? You good?"

"Yeah. Everything's good. We just need to talk about something."

"Al problems?" he asked.

"Nah. I'll tell you when you get here."

"Aight, I'll be there in about fifteen minutes," he told me.

"Bet. I'll be down in the office," I said and hung up.

I walked into my office and rolled a fresh blunt. I put the blunt up to my lips and lit it. Ever since I'd been let out of jail, I made sure I kept my gun and a fresh blunt in my reach. Niggas wanted to take my life and my freedom, so my paranoia seemed to triple. It had gotten so bad that I found myself peeking through the blinds at night and holding my gun like Malcolm X just to make sure there wasn't an unmarked car trying to scope out my house.

As the smoke filled my lungs, I started to calm myself down enough to start really putting some shit together in my head. I had been tellin' everyone that I was going to handle shit to keep the peace and buy myself some time, but I had only figured out bits and pieces of what I wanted to do.

"What's up?"

I turned around to see Blaze walking in through the door.

"Hey."

"What you lookin' at?"

"Nothin," I said as I turned to walk away from the window.

"What's up? You said you wanted to talk to me."

"Sit down," I said as I poured myself a glass of Henny and took a sip of it.

"I already don't like this shit," he said, shaking his head.

"That detective followed Raquel in the mall today."

"What?"

"Yeah." I nodded.

"I'm tellin' you, Law. Just let me handle his ass and all of our problems will go away. Put a bullet hole the size of a fucking golf ball right in the back of his head. All you gotta do is point his ass out, and I'll spray that nigga."

"Nigga, if you kill a fucking cop, that's only going to make our problems worse! You already know if you cut the head off one of them mothafuckas, another one will grow right back."

"You right. So what you gon' do? What did he say to her? Anything?"

"He said he wants her to testify."

"Against you?"

"Yeah." I sighed and shook my head.

"Aw, shit, but she ain't gon' do it, right?"

"Nah, but that's not gonna stop him from coming at her," I said as I passed him my blunt.

Blaze nodded, and the two of us sat in silence for a few minutes, passing the blunt back and forth until he spoke up.

"I think I know a way that'll stop him from coming around."

"For the last fucking time, nigga, we are not killin' a cop!"

Blaze chuckled and coughed.

"That's not what the fuck I was gonna say, nigga."

"Oh. Then what's up?"

"I know this is probably the last shit you wanna do, but just hear me out first."

"I'm listening."

"You gotta marry her," Blaze told me as he passed my blunt back to me.

"I gotta what?"

"Yeah. I know the shit sounds crazy, but if she's your wife, they can't make her testify against you or no crazy shit like that. That makes you and me safe since she was the only witness to the shit, and it makes her safe, too."

"I don't know, Blaze. Marriage is the furthest thing from my mind right now."

"Yeah, I know, but just think about it at least. We're talking about your freedom here, and if this fucking detective is really trying to go hard to lock you up, you at least should be ready and have all your shit straight, you know?"

"Yeah, I feel you. I don't know. I'll think about that shit."

"Yeah, do that."

"Thanks, though."

"No problem. You already know that no matter what, I'm gonna hold you down. But um... since I got you here right now, there's something else I need to tell you ..."

"What's up?" I asked, as I took another pull from my blunt.

"It's about Mom, yo... She's sick."

* * *

Blaze

"What do you mean she's sick?" Law asked me.

I sighed and shook my head. I knew I was about to go against everything my mom wanted me to do, but I just didn't feel right holding that type of shit back from my brother any more.

"She told me not to tell you, but I thought you needed to know."

"What the fuck do you mean she's sick, Blaze? Like she got a cold or something? Is she in the hospital? What's up?"

"It's cancer, Law ..."

Law took the blunt away from his mouth and stared at me. I knew he wouldn't take the news well, but I didn't think he'd completely shut down. The two of us sat in silence for almost five minutes before he started shaking his head back and forth.

"How long have you known that shit?" he asked.

"She told me the day of your wedding. That's why I wasn't there when the cops fucking came to get you. She called me and asked me to come to the house because she had to talk to me about something. When I got there, she told me that she was sick."

"How sick is she though?"

"She's dying," I told him.

"No! Fuck no! No the fuck she's not! I don't ever want to hear that shit come out of your fucking mouth again, nigga!" he yelled.

"I know it's not the shit you wanna hear right now, but she told me she's not doing the treatments. She's not doin' none of that shit. It's stage three, and she's done, Law. She's not fighting the shit no more."

"Why the fuck she ain't want me to know, huh? Why the fuck she tell you instead of me!" he yelled.

"She said she knew what we could take, and you weren't in a place that you would be able to take the shit the way she needed you to." I shrugged.

"Get the fuck outta here with that shit, nigga."

"I'm just telling you what she told me. That's all. Just don't say shit to her. She was for real about me not telling you until she was ready."

"Nah, fuck that. She's taking the treatment. I'm going to move her ass right into the guest house and make sure we have doctors and nurses on call around the clock if we need to. Whatever she needs, she's gonna get it. I'm not lettin' her give up. We already lost Wolfe and Pops. I'll be damned if we lose her, too."

I nodded. I could see how fucked up he was about the news. His mind couldn't process it all just like mine couldn't when she

55

first told me. Law was angry, and I knew that he had a valid point about not wanting to lose our mom, but at the same time, she was a grown ass woman. She was going to do what she wanted to do.

"I'm not losing her. I'm fucking not. I'm not losin' nobody fucking else in this mothafucking family! You hear me!" he yelled as he drove his index finger into the wood on the desk.

I watched Law put the blunt down and cover his face with his hands. I could feel my throat tightening every time I tried to swallow. It was gon' kill me if he broke down. Neither of us could afford to be weak or show any type of emotion, not even to each other. I walked over and patted him on the back.

"We gon' be good, man. Everything is gon' work out for the best," I told him, trying to sound as positive as possible.

Law nodded and lifted his head. He grabbed his glass and downed the remaining liquor in one gulp. He got up and walked over to pour himself another glass.

"Yo, pour me one while you over there," I told him.

He nodded and poured me a glass after he refilled his own, then handed it to me. The both of us sat in silence and drank.

"You gon' be good?" I asked.

"Yeah. I'm straight." He nodded.

Instead of responding, I nodded back to him.

"I'm about to head down to the strip club tonight. You tryna roll with me?" I asked.

"Nah, you go ahead, though. I'm gon' sit here and get my fucking thoughts straight."

"Aight." I nodded. "You sure you good though?"

"Yeah."

I chugged the rest of the Hennessy in my glass and put it on the edge of his desk then left him sitting in the office to collect his thoughts. I went to my room and got in the shower to get ready to blow some bands on some strippers. I walked out of the house wearing nothing but a bowtie, a pair of black jeans and some black Jordan's. The rest of my body was wrapped in diamonds from my ears to my chest and both my wrists. My body was looking like I had just flown in from Iceland, but I didn't give a fuck how flashy I was or what broke niggas I offended. A nigga needed to unwind.

When I got inside the club, I headed straight for the bar. By the time I had been in there for an hour, I was lit. I was in the club, acting like a straight savage, standing on couches, pouring Henny into the strippers' mouths like a cognac fountain. I was acting a fool and wasn't nobody gon' stop me. I was in there blowing money fast like Big Meech, paying for tuition, braces, down payments on cars and apartments and some more shit. I didn't give a fuck.

I walked around the club with a bottle of Henny attached to my hand like always. I was looking for someone to slide into for the night and release some tension. Shit was getting too real at home, and I needed a break. That's when I saw her. She was a brown-skinned beauty. She was petite and couldn't have weighed more than a buck ten, but she carried all of her weight in her ass. Her waist was tiny, and her breasts were medium-sized. Her lips were just as juicy as her thighs. Her hair was dripping down her back. I didn't give a fuck if it was fake. The shit looked good on her.

I stood there, admiring her from afar while she popped her ass to the music. The Henny and the weed were getting the best of me, and I was stuck in a trance. I was swimming in a sea of a hundred freaks willing to do whatever if the money was right, but once my eyes locked on her, she was all I saw. A nigga had tunnel vision. Just looking at her had me scheming on how I could take her home with me. I didn't give a fuck if she had a man because I knew my game was solid. It had never let me down before. I couldn't let her walk by without shooting my shot. I wasn't a thirsty ass nigga, but I wanted her bad. After the song went off, I made my way over to her.

"I'm tryna get a dance," I told her.

"Gimme some of your Henny, and I got you," she said.

I passed her the bottle in my hand, and she took a swig out of it and swallowed it like a straight G.

"Damn, I see you." I nodded as I took the bottle back from her.

"Yeah, I can definitely hold my own liquor." She nodded.

"What's your name?"

"Nevaeh. It's Heaven spelled backward."

"Heaven, huh?"

"Yeah." She nodded.

"Well, I'm Blaze."

"Blaze, huh? I thought you were gonna say your name was Ice or something because you are really shining," she said as she lifted my chain and then let it fall back against my bare chest.

"Thank you. You lookin' better than better tonight. You got all the niggas in here ready to pay all your bills, huh?"

"Somethin' like that." She smirked. "Funny thing about that is I don't see nobody else but you."

"Oh, I see you runnin' game."

"Who me?" She giggled.

"Yeah, you. Don't worry about it, though. It's cute. I like it."

I turned the bottle up to my lips again and then passed it to her.

"Damn, I see you holdin' your liquor, too," she said.

"Yeah, I can definitely do that. Ask them bitches 'bout me," I said, flashing her ass a wide smile.

"Damn, you really feelin' yourself. I can see all thirty-two teeth," she joked.

"Oh, you got jokes, huh?"

"Yeah. Maybe I do." She shrugged and then took another swig.

Heaven and I went round for round, taking shots of Henny until I knew she was about to throw up. I had no idea how her little body could hold so much liquor. My head was spinning, so I knew she had to be just as lit as I was if not more.

"Yo, but for real, I'm in here all the time, and I've never seen you before. You new or somethin'?" I asked.

"Kinda... I just started here about a week ago."

"Oh, yeah?"

"Yeah." She nodded. "I'm just trying to pay my way through school, you know? This is the quickest way."

"Oh, word? What you goin' to school for?" I asked.

"Criminal justice. I wanna be a lawyer one day."

"Damn, a lawyer, huh? That's what's up." I nodded.

Before she got a reply out, the DJ got on the mic and yelled for a big shout out to all the birthday girls and then dropped the "Birthday Song" by 2 Chainz, and all the females went crazy like it was a brand new song. Heaven started twerking extra hard in front of me, making one ass cheek pop then the other. The harder she twerked, the faster I threw money.

"Damn, girl."

"Gotta do what the song say. It's my birthday." She smiled.

"Oh, for real? Well, then shout out to you, birthday girl."

"Thank you."

"What you want for your birthday?"

"You," She smiled.

"There you go with that game again." I laughed.

She was poppin' her pussy for a nigga like my name was Uncle Luke with the 2 Live Crew. Everything she did had me caught up like a deer in headlights. All I could do was keep picturing every position I was going to fuck her in if she gave me the chance. I didn't even know if I was gonna put a condom on.

"Damn," I said as I bit my lip.

"What?"

"You just lookin' so good. I love how you twerkin' that ass, too."

"Oh, you like that?"

"Yeah, I do. You know what I wanna know?"

"What?"

"I wanna know if you can do that on the dick, though."

"Hmm... Wouldn't you like to know."

"Hell yeah, I would. You keep dancin' like that, you gon' make me tilt that halo of yours tonight." I smirked.

I knew that wasn't nothin' but the Henny talking. I was so faded I could barely stand up.

"You keep tellin' me you want me, but all I hear is words."

"What you mean, girl?"

"I mean, you gotta prove it to me."

I flashed her a smile. All that told me was that I had her, and if I kept playing my cards right, she'd be in my bed before the sun came up.

"What I gotta prove, baby girl?"

"That you want me," she said as she closed her eyes and swayed to the beat.

"Shit, you ain't said nothin'. Bring that ass over here."

Heaven came closer to me and kissed my neck.

"What time you plan on leaving here?" she asked.

"Whatever time you get off," I told her.

She smiled, nodded, and kept right on dancing. Like DMX used to say, "I like my blunts heavily hashed, bitches heavily assed." Heaven fit the description to a T. I just knew her pussy had to be good because it smelled like water. I was down to taste every inch of her body. As the songs went on, I kept getting more and more impatient. I pulled out my phone and looked at the screen to check the time. It was 2:45 a.m.

"You 'bout ready to dip?" I asked her.

"Yeah. I've definitely made enough for the night fucking with you."

"Cool because I'm about ready to start fucking with you," I told her.

"Is that right?" she asked.

"Hell yeah. You want me to fuck you while I'm wearin' my chain?"

"Nope. I want you to fuck me while I wear your chain," she said as she toyed with it.

I smiled and lifted my chain from around my neck and placed it around hers.

"C'mon. Let's go."

"Aight. Let me just change and grab my stuff. I'll be back in a minute."

I nodded and put the bottle up to my lips again and drank the rest of it. Heaven stayed true to her word and came back out of the back room wearing a tank top and a pair of gray joggers that hugged her curves perfectly. She locked arms with me as we walked out of the club.

"You sure you good to drive? I don't know about you, but I'm wavy as fuck," she told me.

"Yeah. I do this shit all the time."

"Just because you do it all the time, don't mean you good."

"I'm good. Trust me."

I unlocked my car, dropped my body into the driver's seat, and started the engine. Before we both knew it, Heaven and I were pulling up to the house. I slammed on the brakes ,and we both jerked forward.

"Damn, my fault." I chuckled.

"At least we made it here safe."

"Aight, cool. Well, my brother and his girl are probably inside, so try not to make too much noise."

"He's inside like he lives here?"

"Yeah. This is his house."

"Why do you live with your brother anyway?" she asked.

"After our brother was killed, we decided it would be best for me to move in with him to keep the family close, you know? But don't get it twisted, I ain't no broke ass nigga. I can hold my own," I assured her.

"Keep the family close... I get it." She nodded.

"Aight, let's go."

Heaven was doing way more talking than I wanted her to, but a part of me didn't mind it. We both got out of the car and walked into the house. I didn't stop until we got upstairs to my room.

"Wow, this is nice," she said as she walked in.

I nodded and then closed and locked the door behind me. "Thank you."

As soon as I turned back to face her, she dropped down to her knees in front of me. I smiled. We were finally about to get to the thing I had been wanting to do since I first saw her. I could already tell she was going to be a problem. It was going to be Heaven versus Hell in my room. Heaven crawled closer to me and pulled out my dick. She started stroking it with her right hand while she stared at it.

"Ain't no way you fittin' all this in your mouth," I told her.

"You sure about that?"

"Let me see then."

I had been envisioning what her lips would look like wrapped around my dick all night, and I was ready to see what that mouth was about. Without saying another word, Heaven started deep throating me.

"Oh shit," I said as I sucked in air through my teeth.

Her ass was a straight up freak. I grabbed the back of her head and started guiding her head down on my dick. I could hear her gagging as my dick touched the back of her throat. She would deep throat until she damn near choked, come up for air, and then go right back down to gurgling on it. I chewed my bottom lip as I watched her suck my dick like a true professional. Heaven slid my dick out of her mouth and rubbed it against her hard nipples and looked up at me.

"I wanna feel your tongue, baby."

"You wanna feel my tongue, huh?"

"Mmm, yes."

"Tell daddy how bad you want to feel this tongue."

"I wanna feel it real bad," she moaned.

I pushed her down on the bed and pulled her G-string to the side. I lifted her legs up in the air and kissed the stretch marks on the back of her thighs, which made her shiver. I kissed her clit and then sucked on it gently. I could already feel her legs trembling, and I hadn't even put my long tongue to good use. I started licking up and down her entire pussy all the way down to her asshole. I curved my tongue, and I licked in circles and flicked her clit.

"Oooohhhh shit!" She squealed as she squeezed her ass cheeks together.

My entire face was wet from tongue swimming in her wet ass pussy; I needed a boat. The more I sucked and flicked her clit with my tongue, the more she squirmed. I could tell the slurping sounds of my tongue drove her wild.

"Mmmm, fuckkkkkk!" she moaned, as she clenched her thighs together, locking my head in between them.

I quickly opened her legs and sat up. I pushed both of her legs up by her head and watched my dick slide in and out of her juicy ass pussy. I let my spit drop down to her pussy, and I rubbed her clit. Heaven's pussy had my whole bed wet instantly.

"Oh my God!" she screamed.

"Yeah, that's right, baby girl. Call on 'em."

My dick was sliding in and out of her pussy with ease. Her shit was wetter than water. I pressed my hands into her rib cage and held her tight as I drilled deep into her stomach.

"Mmm... shit... Blaze!"

I wrapped my hand around her throat and fucked her harder until I knew she came for the first time.

"Oooh shit, Blaze. Baby, I'm coming!"

"Cum on this dick, Heaven," I told her.

I adjusted my bowtie around my neck and glanced down at the watch around my wrist. As long as I still had something on my body, I was good. I wasn't fucking her ass completely naked. That was some shit that happened only when you loved a bitch. There was no love involved in anything that we were doing.

Heaven climbed on top of me and started riding the shit out of my dick, bouncing up and down. Heaven even twerked on my dick while I was inside of her. I reached up and shoved my fingers in her mouth to watch her suck on them.

"Mmm," she moaned.

I slid my fingers out of her mouth and held her throat with both hands as she rode my dick. I was loving the way she was riding my dick. She moved her hips like she was straight off the boat from the islands. Heaven arched her back as I held her up by her thighs and pumped my dick into her while she was on top of me. I reached around and slapped her ass.

"Yeah, you ride this dick. Get that nut, Heaven," I told her as I slapped her ass again.

I watched Heaven continue to ride me until she came again. Then I lifted her off of me to change positions. I got up and stood on the side of my bed and pulled her to the edge. I slapped her ass, and she instantly started twerking for me. I mounted her from behind to fuck her doggy style. She was bent over just right and was breathing just as heavy as I was.

"Mmm, fuck! Stick your finger in my ass!" she moaned.

"Damn, bitch, you nasty," I said as I flashed her a devious smile and put my thumb in her tight ass. "You want me to stick my dick in there, too?"

"Mmm... Yesss, baby. Stick your big ass dick in my ass."

I slid my thumb out and watched her arch her back. I spit on my hand and rubbed it on her asshole then slowly slid my dick inside her ass.

"Goddamn!" I groaned as I slowly pumped into her.

"Mmmm... fuckkkkkkkk," she moaned as she started rubbing her clit.

"Yeah, that's right. Play with that fucking pussy."

I locked my arms underneath her legs and lifted her petite body up off the bed. Then I put her in a full nelson as I slammed into her pussy from behind. She could barely take it, but I didn't care. I kept her in that position and continued fucking her all over my room from the bed to the floor to the fucking ceiling. I was knocking her pussy walls down like dominoes. All I could hear was Heaven moaning, telling me to go deeper. I was in the zone, and I could feel myself about to nut.

"Mmm, shit," I groaned.

"Mmm... Yes, baby. Are you about to cum?"

"Mmhm."

"Yeah. That's right, daddy. I want you to cum all in this pussy."

"You want me to cum all in this pussy?" I asked through gritted teeth.

"Mmmm... yesssss!"

I pumped into her a few more times and then came inside of her a little before pulling out and shooting the rest of my nut on her ass and pussy.

"Shit!" I groaned and then collapsed beside her.

* * *

I woke up the next morning with my head swimming. It was so heavy I could barely lift it off the pillow. I slowly rolled over and my eyes caught the back of Heaven's head and the rest of her naked body. I barely remembered the night we spent together, but I knew the shit was amazing. A yawn slipped out of my mouth as I sat up. Heaven stirred in her sleep and turned over to face me.

"Good morning," she said.

"Mornin'." I nodded.

Without saying another word, she sat up and started getting dressed. I was glad I didn't have to spell it out to her. It was the first time I had ever let a girl spend the night with me, but we were both so faded I didn't even remember falling asleep. I laid back against the bed and watched her put her clothes back on and put her long hair in a low ponytail.

"I should get going," she said as she looked at me.

"Aight, bet." I nodded. "You need me to call you an Uber or something?"

"Nah, I got it. One said it'll be here in about seven minutes."
She nodded.

"Cool. Uh, can I get your number before you go?" I asked.

"Yeah. Lemme see your phone."

"I don't even know where that shit is right now," I told her.

"Check your pants pocket. It's probably in there."

I nodded and turned my attention down to the floor to scan it for my pants. I locked eyes on them and slowly got up to fish around for my phone. When I found it, I handed it to her.

"Here," I said.

I watched Heaven type in her number and hand it back to me.

"There you go."

"This better not be no fake number either, girl."

"It's not. I promise." She laughed.

"Good, and don't be tryna act all fake and bougie when you see me out either," I joked.

"Shut up. I won't. I'm not like that."

I looked at her and smiled.

"What?" she asked.

"Those shots of Henny turned your ass to a monster."

"You were goin' hard off that Hen, too." She nodded. "So you were a monster yourself."

"Yeah. It's definitely a sunshades and Tylenol type of day. Last night was real as fuck," I said as I laid back against the pillow.

"I hope that means you enjoyed yourself."

"Oh, I definitely did. If I didn't, I would've never asked for your number." I laughed.

"Oh. My Uber driver is downstairs. I guess I'll talk to you whenever you decide to call me or if I see you at the club again. Whichever comes first." She shrugged.

"Definitely." I nodded.

"Oh, and here you go," she said as she slid my chain over her head and laid it beside me on the bed.

I chuckled a bit and nodded.

"Thank you."

Heaven left and closed the door behind her, and I rolled over onto my side. All I wanted to do was sleep and get high. I knew that was going to be on the only thing to bring me back around after a night of drowning in Hennessy and Heaven's pussy.

CHAPTER FIVE

Ian

I f there was one thing I hated, it was fucking secrets, especially when it came to my family. I had done a lot of thinking on what Blaze had told me, including the part about my mother being sick. It was hard enough fighting a case and trying to protect everything I loved. I didn't think I could handle losing my mother, too. My mother was the first person to ever tell me that she knew I was different the moment I came into this world.

When I was younger, I thought life would be easy. Growing up, the three of us didn't have to worry about shit. Our father provided everything we ever needed. We had a roof over our heads, two parents, and food on the table every night. Shit, as far as I was concerned, that was the lap of luxury right there. That is until I got older and hungrier and not for food. Ain't nothing free in this world, and if anything, the streets will teach you that the quickest. I watched Wolfe out in the streets with his boys, playing ball, shooting guns, and I couldn't wait for the first chance to squeeze a trigger.

When I got to high school, everything changed. Hanging around Wolfe, I learned how to sag my jeans just right like the niggas in New York. My mother noticed everything from the moment my grades started slipping. It didn't matter how many hours she spent working, she always seemed to be two steps ahead of me. She would always find the cigarettes in my jacket pocket and the dime bags of weed in my jeans. It didn't matter; she was hip.

My mother came from a crime family. She married my father, who was the head of a gang, when she was eighteen. If you ask me, their marriage was strategic. My mother had the connect that my father needed to really start pushing weight and bringing in the money they both wanted to make their dreams come true. That connect was Alastair Moreno. He had been dealing with her family for years. My mother was the link between Alastair and my father.

The night my father was killed broke my mother's heart. She went into hiding after that and vowed to lay low and live out the rest of her days in peace and let us take over what our father had left behind. Once Wolfe was killed, my mother damn near went crazy. I didn't even want to think about what I'd do if she died. I wanted to tell Raquel about my mother, but I already had too much weighing on me when it came to her.

I couldn't believe that the only way to get the police off my back and Raquel's was if I married her. The last thing I wanted to do was think about marriage after the bullshit I'd just went through. I knew I loved her, but I just didn't know if that was enough to actually marry her. The question I kept asking myself was could I live without her? From the moment I saw her, I knew I had to have her, so I got her. I almost killed Dallas when I saw him at the penthouse. Just thinking about her being with another nigga, any nigga, made my blood boil. Raquel had a nigga catching feelings. In my eyes, she was already wifey. I turned my attention to Raquel as she walked into the kitchen.

"Hey."

"Hey," I said, shooting her a half smile.

"What's on your mind?"

"Why you ask that?"

"You look stressed like you got a lot of shit on your mind."

"I do."

"Then let's unload it. What's up?" she asked as she sat on top of the counter.

I leaned against the island and looked at her.

"You care about a nigga, Raquel?"

"What kind of question is that?"

"A real one."

"Yes, I do. Of course, I do."

"I hear you, but how much though?"

"I mean, I love you, Law. I don't know how else to explain it." She shrugged.

"But you see the disconnect I have with that shit, right? I mean, I had a fucking fiancée not even a month ago tell me the exact same shit, and I just knew her ass was a rider. Then you come into my life, you turn my shit upside down, and I don't know. I just don't know what to do with what you're saying."

"Law, I mean, I get that you're hurt, but I didn't come back here to be Shiya's replacement or live in her shadow!"

"Nah, I'm not saying that. That's not what I'm saying at all. It's just... you gotta understand why I'm more hesitant. Shit, you should be too. Before you met me, you were ready to marry the love of your life."

"So, you're hesitant to tell me that you love me, but you're not hesitant to fuck me, right?" she asked, folding her arms across her chest.

"That's not what I'm tryna say," I sighed.

By the tone in her voice, I already knew that things were going left, and I didn't want to deal with it.

"You know I'd go the distance for you, Law."

"Do you really mean that?"

"I do." She nodded.

"Then marry me..."

"What?"

"If you marry me, then they can't make you testify against me in court. That keeps you and me safe."

Raquel exhaled slowly and shook her head.

"No."

"Fuck do you mean no?" I asked, standing straight up.

"You heard me. I said no."

The room fell silent, and all I heard was the humming of the refrigerator behind me. I shook my head. I didn't know how else to react. I couldn't believe what I was hearing. Raquel was the first woman to ever tell me no before.

"I want you, Raquel."

"No, you don't. You didn't just ask me to marry you because you want me. You asked me because you want me to save your ass. That wasn't even a real proposal. I deserve better than that!"

"How are you going to tell me what I want?" I asked, pointing to my chest.

Raquel hopped off the edge of the counter and stepped closer to me.

"You may want me, Law, but you want this life more!" she said, expanding her arms to reach as wide and far as they could. "If this is the life you want... the life of a street king or a kingpin or whatever, then I'm not who you need to be with because this isn't the life I want!"

"So, what are you saying?"

"I'm saying you need to decide. It's either the life with the glitz and the glam and the bitches falling at your feet and the money, or it's me... just plain ol' me."

I stared at Raquel in silence. It was hard to trust anything anybody said to me. Everybody had ulterior motives and ill intentions. All I heard from Raquel was that if we ever were officially married, I'd have to follow her rules. I wasn't feelin' that shit. I'd never been that type of nigga. She needed to know that loving me was complicated.

"Raquel, look ..."

"No, you look. You don't get it, do you? I don't want your money. I don't want your crown or the jewelry or the cars. I just want you, a watered-down version of you. Can you honestly stand here and tell me that you're going to give it to me? Huh? Are you going to give me what I want if I agree to marry you?"

I shook my head. I wanted her to be devious or a scammer so bad sometimes. Anything that would make it harder to love her, but she wasn't. She was Raquel, genuine ass Raquel, and I loved her. When I didn't respond immediately, she started talking again.

"I want to curl up with you on a sofa in the middle of the afternoon. I want to lean against the kitchen countertop and talk to you about your day, not wonder whether or not you're coming home in once piece every time you leave out that fucking front door."

"I know my edges are sharp, Raquel, but it's hard to put a stop to something that's already been in motion for so long. There are things I have to do first. That's all. You're just going to have to trust me," I told her.

"Things like what? Huh? And when you're gone, then what? Ain't no coming back! Then what am I gonna do, huh? I don't wanna live my life like that, Law, and telling you I'd marry you is me signing up to do just that."

"I'm not going anywhere, Raquel."

She sucked her teeth and shook her head.

"I find that real hard to believe seeing as though you were hauled off to jail in the blink of an eye not too long ago. You can't even tell me you love me, and it's because you don't! If you did, you wouldn't have a problem saying it!"

I sighed. She just didn't understand that I was trying to protect her. That's what happened when people always thought with their hearts instead of their heads. Shit would get lost in translation. All she could focus on were the words I didn't say and not the words I was actually saying. If she was listening, she could've heard me tell her I loved her in a hundred different ways without actually saying those three words. I had to laugh out of pure frustration.

"What the fuck are you laughing for, Law? The shit isn't funny!"

"You just don't get it," I said, shaking my head.

"What is it? What don't I get? Explain it to me."

"Nothing," I said, shaking my head. "I'll just talk to you about it later."

"What? No! See? That's that shit right there. That's your defense mechanism you always pull away whenever shit gets too deep and don't want to talk anymore. You always leave! Stop running from me, Law!"

"I'll stop running when you start listening, Raquel."

"What are you talking about? I am listening! I always listen to you."

"Then why can't you hear me tell you that I love you without saying those words? Your mind is so fucked up and focused on the wrong shit that you can't hear anything else!"

"Law, I ..."

"Nah, like I told you, we'll talk about this shit some other time. I'm done right now."

I walked out of the kitchen and went to my office. I closed and locked the door behind me and walked over to pour myself a glass of Hennessy and roll a blunt. I sat alone and stared at the bottle in front of me. If that bottle could talk, I didn't know what the fuck it would say. I was just trying to be on my own time, doing my own thing. I was on some fuck everybody shit. I knew I didn't need or want anybody near me in that moment. I just needed to collect my thoughts and keep to myself. I must've been crazy to want to try and ever walk down the aisle again, but she was worth it, and once I handled everything I had to do, I was going to make sure she knew it.

* * *

Nashiya

After spending days at the hotel sulking, I decided to get out and get some fresh air. I hadn't been in contact with Law to get any of my things, so buying some clothes was one of the first things on my to-do list. I went into the mall and dropped into Zara, one of my favorite stores, when I saw Raquel fucking shopping in her own little world.

"Well, if it isn't Little Miss Perfect," I said as I walked up behind her.

She turned around to look at me and immediately balled up her face. I hated the sight of her dumb ass. She shocked me when she turned around and continued to shop, ignoring me.

"Oh, so you don't hear me, huh?"

"No. I don't."

"You wanted to be me so bad, didn't you?" I asked her.

That comment got her to turn around. She looked at me and scoffed.

"Be you? What? You're crazy, Shiya. You seriously need help."

"Bitch, you ain't seen crazy yet. I told your ass from day one not to fuck with my man or my money, and what did you do? Huh? You tried to take both from me."

"I didn't *try* to do anything. It's not my fault Law saw you for what you really are before he made the biggest mistake of his life by marrying you!"

"Oh, sweetheart, that's where you're wrong. The biggest

mistake Law ever made was playing me, and we all see how that turned out for his ass." I snickered.

"Please! Law told me exactly who Dallas was! You were playing me from the very beginning, and I was a fool for falling for it. I wouldn't be surprised if he was already aware of whatever little scheme it is that you have going on in your twisted head."

I snickered again. She was nothing but a child in my eyes. I couldn't take her ass seriously. I was shocked. There was a little more bark to her bite than I expected, but it wasn't making any waves compared to mine.

"A little scheme, huh?" I asked.

"You heard what I said, Nashiya."

"Oh, you called me by my government name. You must be big mad!" I laughed and brushed past her, making sure I bumped her shoulder. "You ain't seen nothin' yet."

I walked out of the store and left her standing there. Just seeing Raquel had my blood boiling at a rate that I knew was hazardous to my health and hers. It took everything in me not to strangle her right in the middle of the clothing store. After our encounter, I was too pissed off to even think about shopping.

"Fucking bitch," I mumbled.

I pulled my phone out and pressed Law's name to see if I could pick up my things. Each call I made, he sent straight to voicemail. I didn't want to just show up at the house, but then again, I didn't really give a fuck. Who was going to fight me or stop me? Raquel? I hopped in my car and rode over to the house. When I pulled into the driveway, I saw both Law and Blaze's cars outside. I shook my head as I shut the engine off and got out of my car. Instead of ringing the doorbell, I tried to use my key, but the lock had been changed.

"Shit," I mumbled.

I tossed my keys in my Chanel bag and saw the gun inside, resting at the bottom. I quickly closed my purse and pressed the large doorbell repeatedly until I heard someone unlock it on the other end.

"Shiya, what the fuck are you doing here?" Blaze asked me when he opened the door.

"Hey, Blaze."

"You already know we ain't on no kumbaya shit over this way, so it's probably best if you turn your ass around and go back to wherever the fuck you came from before Law sees you."

"Fuck all that. I just came to get my stuff."

Blaze sighed and shook his head.

"Wait right here," he told me and then closed the door in my face.

I sucked my teeth and screwed up my forehead when the door slammed in front of me. Then I reached out to turn the knob and let my damn self into the house. When I closed the door behind me, I saw Law walking down the stairs. My breath hitched. I hadn't seen or heard from him since he pulled that bullshit at our wedding. He still looked so damn good to me, even if he was only wearing a wife beater and a pair of basketball shorts. He stopped at the second to last step when he saw me.

"What the fuck are you doing here?" he asked.

"I just came to get my shit, Law. That's all."

"Yeah? Well, that's too bad. I tossed that shit."

"What the fuck do you mean you tossed that shit? Where the fuck is all my stuff, Law?"

"I bagged all that shit up and threw it out."

"Why the fuck would you do that!" I yelled.

"I can do whatever the fuck I want. You should know that by now. Now, get the fuck out of my house before I throw you out," he said.

"Oh, let me guess. Raquel's not here to fight your battles?"

"She ain't here."

"Oh, I know that. I just hope that means you came to your senses and kicked that weak ass bitch to the curb."

"Nah, that's what I did with your ass."

My nostrils flared as we both stood in the foyer, grilling the hell out of each other. I wanted to scream, fight, break, and shoot everything inside that damn house. I clenched my bag tighter out of frustration. If his ass only knew what I was capable of, he'd tread lightly around me. I didn't take lightly to all the shit talking and threats. His brother, Wolfe, tried that shit with me, and he learned that the hard way.

I was down on South Beach one day, doing what I did best, spending Law's money, when I ran into Dallas. It wasn't like we'd ever really lost touch. I had just distanced myself from him and every other nigga from my past when I got with Law. He told me that he'd gotten a new number and told me how good I was looking, really trying to gas me up. The two of us stood outside the MAC store laughing and joking for a bit. Then he gave me his number, and we parted ways. At first, I didn't have any intentions on using it. For what? I had a man who did any and everything I'd ever asked of him. I was good. I tucked my phone back in my purse, and I went on about my business.

The next day, I was in the living room flipping through channels when the doorbell rang. I got up and walked over to open it for Law's brother, Wolfe.

"Hey, Wolfe. What's up?"

"Same shit, different day. Is my brother here?" he asked.

"Nah. Not at the moment. What's up?"

"Good. I need to holla at you anyway," he told me.

"Okay... About what?"

"I saw you yesterday."

"Okay... Saw me where?"

"In South Beach. You forgot I got a spot out there, right? I saw you talkin' to Dallas Price, Nashiya. How the fuck do you even know that nigga?"

"He's just an old friend, okay? That's it," I said, shrugging it off.

"That's it, huh?"

"Yeah, that's it."

"Now, does my brother know this?"

I stood there silently and didn't say anything to him.

"*That's exactly what I thought. You already know we got beef with them niggas, and you gon' be out in fucking public chattin' it up with that mothafucka? What the fuck is really up with you, bitch? You think I'm stupid or something?*"

"*I'm telling you, Wolfe. What you think you saw was nothin'.*"

"*So, I ain't see that nigga put his number in your phone either, huh?*"

I sighed and chewed my bottom lip. There was nothing else I could say. I was caught up.

"*You want me to delete the shit? Cool. It's done. Say no more.*"

"*Man, fuck deleting it. The damage is already done. You need to tell Law before I do and fuck all this shit up for you. Ain't gon' be no more blowin' bags and plastic fucking surgery or none of that shit, bitch. I'll make sure my brother sends your ass back to stealin' from fucking Jimmy Jazz and DTLR.*"

"*Are you fucking threatening me, Wolfe?*" *I asked.*

"*Nah. No threat, Shiya. See? What that is right there is a fucking promise. I'm giving you the opportunity to be straight with my brother first, but if you don't tell him, you better be fucking sure I will,*" *he said as he turned to leave.*

I stood there, trembling. I slammed the door behind him and let out the loudest yell out of pure anger. I could feel my heart racing faster and faster. I didn't know what the fuck I was going to do. All I could do was panic. I ran back into the living room and grabbed my phone to find Dallas's number in my contacts. I pressed the button to call him and paced the living room floor until he answered.

"*Hello? Who dis?*"

"*It's me... Bird...*"

A week later, Wolfe's ass was killed. It served his ass right for fishing around in my fucking business in the first place. I had to do what I had to do to protect what was mine, and Law may have been Wolfe's brother, but he was my man. Law had a real hard time with the news at first. I'd never seen him so depressed. He almost went crazy over the loss of his older brother, and I understood that. I would've been a wreck if I would've lost my older sister the way he lost Wolfe. So, I did what any devoted female would do for her fiancé; I took care of him. I waited on him hand and foot, all while planting the seed in his mind that Wolfe was power hungry and was making moves behind his back, and that's what got him killed.

I snapped out of my trance when I saw Law brush past me and walk into his office.

"Get the fuck out of my house, Shiya, before I throw your fucking ass out on your neck. This the last time I'm sayin' this shit."

"You know what? Fuck you, Law! I been knew your ass wasn't shit! That's why I ain't shit right along with you! See how you fucking like it!" I said as I followed him back into his office.

If his ass wanted to argue, I was going to argue right along with him. I didn't give a fuck. I took a step back when Law turned around and aimed a gun at my forehead.

"That's your fucking problem, bitch. You mistook a real nigga for just another street nigga, and I'm about to show you the error in your ways. Sit the fuck down."

I put my hands in the air and slowly walked over to sit in a chair across from his desk. I could feel beads of sweat starting to develop on my forehead. All I needed to do was distract him enough so that I could reach in my purse and pull out my own gun. He had to know I wasn't going to lie down easily.

"Whatever, nigga. Yeah, I'm fucked up, but I ain't as fucked up as you!" I spat.

"Get the fuck outta here. The fuck did I ever do to you, huh? I bought you any and everything you wanted. I put that big ass rock on your finger because I thought you was a fucking loyal bitch, and you played me. You don't love no nigga but your fucking self, bitch!"

"Fuck are you talking about, Law? I was ten toes down in the ground for you. It wasn't until that fucking bitch, Raquel, came around and started fucking shit up for us!"

"Oh, so Raquel is the reason you ain't tell me that you knew

Dallas? Raquel is the reason why... You know what? Never mind. I'm doing way too much fucking talking. Get the fuck up," he said as he released the safety on the gun.

My heart started racing as I struggled to settle the trembling in my legs so that I could stand up.

"Law, please. Just let me explain."

"Explain what, bitch? Everything is your fucking fault! You the reason why these fucking cops are on my back! You ain't shit but a thirsty ass bitch! You was mad because I beat you at your own game, so you plotted to take everything I fucking had, and you failed! You said you was with me, and you wasn't. You said you was about a nigga, and you wasn't. You said you loved a nigga, and you lied. I should've left your dusty ass with the broke bitch body you had on you when I fucking met you!"

I watched Law struggle inside himself on whether he was going to pull the trigger or not. It was written all over his face. I had never seen that shit before. That either meant one of two things. Either he still loved me, or he was going to make me suffer.

"I'm going to ask you this shit one time, and one time only. Did you go to the police to set me up for that Damien shit?"

"Law, I—"

"It's a yes or no fucking question, Nashiya."

When I didn't respond, Law stepped closer to me and put the gun up to my lips.

"Since you don't wanna open your mouth, I'm gon' open it for you."

I slowly opened my mouth, and he put the tip of the gun inside it.

"That's what you like, right?"

I kept my eyes focused on his finger that was wrapped around the trigger. Just when Law was about to pull it, there was a knock on the door. Blaze busted in, and I took a sigh of relief.

"Don't do that shit, Law. Not here. Not right now. We got bigger problems," he said.

"What?"

"That fucking Detective Mason is downstairs."

Law pulled the gun out of my mouth and tucked it behind his back.

"Man, fuck!" he yelled. "Take her ass around the back, and get her the fuck outta here while I deal with him."

As Law walked out of the room, Blaze grabbed me by arm and yanked me out of Law's office through the kitchen and out the garage.

"Thank you," I said as I wiped my face.

"Fuck are you thanking me for? I didn't do shit to protect you. I did that shit for my brother. The next time you thinkin' about goin' to the police about some shit, you better make sure you have your fucking facts straight when you tryna snitch. I pulled that trigger once, and I'll do it again with no hesitation, bitch."

Blaze pushed me out through the garage door and I ran to my car. There was a part of me that wanted to pull out my gun and put a bullet in Law and Blaze, but when my eyes landed on the police car in the driveway, I quickly put that thought away. I hopped in my car and sped off. It might've been over for Law, but it wasn't over for me.

CHAPTER SIX

Ian

I went around to the front and opened the door. Low and behold, it was the fucking detective standing on the other side.

"Can I help you?" I asked.

"This is a nice house you have here, Mr. Calloway. What exactly is it that you do again?"

"I mind my business. Fuck are you doing at my house?"

"So, the big court date is coming up. Are you ready?" he asked.

"What is it that you want, Detective? I was in the middle of something important."

"What's that? Trying to cover up another murder, Mr. Calloway?"

"I didn't cover up the first one because I didn't have shit to do with it."

"You know what I found disturbing? Almost funny even?"

"What's that?"

"I did a little investigating on your girlfriend, Raquel. She is your girlfriend, right?"

"What about her?"

"It seems that about a week after she first came down here, someone by the name of Shante Richards tried to file a missing person's report."

"Okay, but you can see that she's not missing with your own eyes, so what's your point?"

"I just find it funny that Miss Valentine witnesses a murder, she calls the police, and then her phone goes dead. She doesn't return home, her friend gets worried, and tries to file a report, but then suddenly, she's riding around Miami with you, the man who she witnessed kill someone in cold blood. You know what I think?"

"What?"

"I think either you've brainwashed that poor girl into thinking you're anything more than a murdering piece of shit, or she's dumber than she looks."

All I could think about in that moment was that I was happy Raquel was out and about and not around to witness Shiya's visit or the detective's either. Everything inside me was still on some straight murder shit. My adrenaline was on a thousand over Shiya's ass, and the detective wasn't making shit any better. I wanted to pull out my gun and unload my entire clip into both of their chests. Who the fuck would really miss either of them?

"Nobody ever told you that jealousy will get you killed?" I asked him.

"Is that a threat, Andreas?" he asked, stepping into my face.

"No, sir. It's not. Now if there is anything else you need from me, feel free to reach out to my lawyer. Until then, get the fuck off my property."

The detective looked me up and down and then stepped back.

"I'll see you in court, and I'm going to make sure I put you away," he told me and turned to head back to his car.

I stood in the doorway and watched him pull off before I closed the door. If it wasn't for Shiya's ass, I wouldn't have any of the problems I did. As far as I was concerned, all she had done when she showed up was pour gasoline on a bridge that she'd already burned with me. She tried to trick me out of my spot and watch me lose it all. Shiya was dead to me, and it was killing her. The shit was written all over her face. She knew exactly what she did. She had started an all-out war, and I was ready to blow any mothafucka straight out of their J's if they even looked at me the wrong way. I was about to fall back into my old ways and become a straight savage.

* * *

Raquel

I was still mad at Law after the last conversation we had. I was just happy that I could come and go as I pleased without anybody losing their shit. When I got home, I went to the room and crawled under the covers for a nap. Just when I had gotten into a good sleep, I heard Law come in the room and close the door.

"When did you get home?" he asked.

I kept my back turned and laid still. I didn't want to talk.

"Oh, so you don't hear me now?" he asked.

Law climbed in the bed behind me and rolled me over onto my back.

"Look at me, Raquel."

I opened my eyes and looked at him. He lifted my shirt up, put his head underneath the covers, and started sucking on my breasts.

"Law, what are you doing?"

"Shh."

He gently sucked on my nipples and then kissed down my

chest, biting at my rib cage. He rubbed on my pussy through my panties, and I slowly opened my legs for him. He pulled my panties to the side and gently flicked my pussy with his long tongue. Just the simplest touch was driving me wild. He ran circles around my clit with his tongue, then looked up at me.

"Are you still mad?"

I looked down at him and nodded. Law smiled and started licking my pussy again. Then he sat up to pull me in to kiss him and stuck his tongue in my mouth.

"Mmm. Taste how sweet your pussy is, Raquel."

I climbed off the edge of the bed and pulled my shirt up over my head. I wasn't wearing a bra, and all I had left on was a skirt and a pair of soaking wet panties.

"Stand up," I told him.

Law stood to his feet, and I dropped down to my knees in front of him. I pulled down his basketball shorts and boxers then took his dick in my mouth. I sucked his dick for a few minutes to get it nice and wet, but he interrupted me.

"Raquel, get up," he said as he tried to take a step backward.

I shook my head as I licked the tip of his dick.

"I said stand up."

"Nope." I smirked.

"Oh, you being hard headed, huh?"

"Maybe."

"When I tell you to listen, you listen," he said as he pulled me to my feet and spun me around.

Within seconds, Law had laid me on my back, lifted my skirt over my hips, pulled my panties to the side, and slid inside of me.

"Mmm... shiiiitttt!" I groaned, as I grabbed hold of the comforter underneath me.

"You wanna be hard headed and shit. Take this hard ass dick," he told me.

"Yeah, baby. Yessss," I moaned.

He pulled out and wiped the wetness from my pussy onto his dick and then slid back inside me.

"Mmm... Look at you creamin'. Cum on daddy's dick all you want."

"Mmm... Yeah."

"Come get on top."

Law laid on his back, and I climbed on top of him. I was getting more used to sex in general, but I definitely took a liking to being on top and riding his dick. As soon as I slid down on his dick, he held his hands underneath my ass and thrust upward into my pussy.

"Oooh shit," I said as I reached back and put my hand on his thigh to slow him down.

"Don't run from this dick, Raquel. Take it. Take all this dick," he said as he pushed faster.

Law grabbed my arms and held onto them so that I couldn't push him away.

"Mmm... Yeah, that's right, baby. Take that shit," he said as he pulled out and slapped his dick against my pussy.

I could barely take all the pleasure, and I could feel a tear coming to my eye. He quickly slid back inside me and held my waist tight as I started to slowly grind my hips. The faster I moved, the closer I felt myself nearing my climax. I started riding him harder and pulling on my right nipple at the same time.

"Ooooh, baby. I'm about to cum! Yesss!"

"You gon' cum for daddy?"

"Yesss!"

"Tell me you'll marry me."

"Yes! I'll marry you, Law!"

"Tell me you want to be my wife, Raquel."

"Yes, yes! I want to be your wife!"

"Mmm, shit," he said as he grabbed my waist tight and came right behind me.

His grip was so tight that I knew I was going to have bruises the next day.

"Damn," I said as I slowly rolled off him and tried to catch my breath.

"*Damn* is right. Come here."

I rolled over and laid on his chest and attempted to cover myself with some of the bed sheets.

"You know you said you'd be my wife, right?" he asked.

"Yup. I know what I said."

"Just checking. But for real though, Raquel, I can't promise you that I'll leave all this shit alone, but I'll seriously consider it once I tie up some loose ends."

"Let me guess; you're not going to tell me what those loose ends are, are you?"

"No," he said, shaking his head. "But I will tell you something else."

"What's that?"

"I found out my mother has cancer, and she's dying."

I quickly sat up and looked at him.

"Oh my God, Law. Are you serious? When did you find out?"

"Not too long ago. She didn't want me to know. She still doesn't know that I do."

"How'd you find out?"

"She told Blaze, and Blaze told me."

"Why do you think she wouldn't want you to know something important like that, though?"

"I don't know." He shrugged. "She said something about knowing what I could handle and when I could handle it. At least that's what he told me she said."

"You haven't talked to her at all?"

"No. I don't know what to say. How do you look the person who gave you life in the eyes, knowing they're dying, and not bring that up? I can't do it right now."

"Law, you can't let your pride get in the way over something as serious as this. She's your mother."

"Are you close with your parents? I know you said you were an only child, but that don't mean y'all were close," he said.

I sat back and reflected for a moment on how to answer his question. It wasn't out of the ordinary for me to go long periods of time without speaking to my parents. They divorced my sophomore year in college and turned my entire life upside down. Being that my father was in the military, he chose to be stationed somewhere else. As far as my mother, I could never tell if she was broken up or happy about her decision to divorce my father. She got so wrapped up in herself that she stopped being someone I could look up to and lean on. The only thing they ever did for me financially was continue to put me through college and give me monetary gifts from time to time like the trip to Miami. Other than that, I couldn't say I really tried hard to keep in touch with my family.

"Not anymore," I told him.

"Why not?"

"They divorced a few years ago, and things just haven't been the same since. I've always been kind of a loner, but all that just really gave a new meaning to the word for me."

Law nodded like he understood.

"The older we get, the more I see that our parents got their own demons to wrestle with."

"Ain't that the truth," I agreed.

"I still want you to meet her, though. My plan is to move her into the guest house and give her around the clock care. I don't know how much longer she has left."

"You can't find out from her doctor?" I asked.

"Nah. She made sure that none of her medical information is released to anyone but her, so even if I did try that, she's probably already made sure the doctors won't tell me anything."

"Damn. Well, I would love to meet her whenever I get the chance."

"Good. I'm about to go downstairs to the kitchen. You want anything?"

"Nah. I'm fine," I told him.

As soon as Law left the room, I grabbed my phone to call Camille. Although he'd just given me some sad news about his mom, I couldn't deny the fact that I was elated that he asked me to marry him again. Still, I had no ring and it wasn't the proposal I'd envisioned, but I loved him, and I realized that was all that mattered.

"Hello?" she answered.

"He asked me to marry him!" I blurted out.

"What!" she screamed into my ear.

"Shh! Lower your voice and calm down," I told her.

"Oh, no. That's it, bitch. I'm on my way down to Miami right now one way, not round trip, and I'm not leaving until I meet this man and you tell me everything. I'm not playing!"

"Camille, girl, no! Listen to me. You cannot come down here now!"

"Whatever! I'm coming, and there's nothing you can do to stop me. Byeeee!" she said and hung up.

I couldn't believe Camille hung up on me like that. I could've strangled her. I left the room to find Law. I had to tell him about Camille to get his thoughts on everything.

"Babe."

"What's up?" he asked with his head inside the refrigerator.

"I need to talk to you about something."

"What's up? What's wrong?"

"My friend is coming down."

"Who? Shante?"

"No... Camille. Hold up. How did you even know about Shante?" I asked as I walked over to him and pulled on his arm.

Law sighed and shook his head.

"It's nothing."

"Stop fucking lying to me, and tell me!"

"Look, Detective Mason came by here about an hour or so ago. He told me that somebody named Shante tried to file a missing person's report after you didn't come back for a week."

"She what?"

"Yeah. That's what he said. I don't know how true it is though."

"Why would he lie about something like that?"

"I don't know." He shrugged.

I huffed as I shook my head.

"Don't worry about it. I'm going to figure it out."

"Just calm down, Raquel. If you don't act like nothing is wrong, neither will she."

"Yeah, I guess you're right."

* * *

Ian

Later that night, I went to Blaze's room and knocked on the door. It was almost midnight, and we had some business to handle. I told him to meet me down at the car in five minutes flat. Once I got in the car, I made sure my gun had all the bullets in it that it could hold and that I had my gloves and my silencer in the glove compartment. When Blaze got in the car, I sped off down the driveway and headed to the warehouse where Alastair's men were supposed to have dropped off our shipment at the warehouse.

Once I went inside and checked that everything was there, we headed to our next stop, Alastair's yacht in Biscayne Bay to pay him an unexpected visit.

"You sure you wanna do this?" Blaze asked me as I pulled up to where Al's yacht was docked.

"I have to." I shrugged. "Just have my back. That's all I need you to do."

"Always, nigga."

Blaze reached over to dap me up, and then I parked the car. I placed my gun in the back of my jeans and headed toward Al's large water home.

"He could be anywhere on that big ass thing," Blaze said, referring to the yacht like it was a cruise ship.

"I'm not worried about him. I'm worried about the mothafuckas that are on this shit with him."

Blaze stopped and put his silencer on his gun, and I did the same.

"Guess it's about to be lights out for their asses then." He shrugged.

We casually walked over the small bridge that took us from land and onto the boat when Al's large, Hispanic guard that always monitored who came on and off the boat stopped us.

"Law? What are you doing here so late?" he asked.

"I didn't know you knew me by name, man. What's up?" I asked, dapping him up. "Al didn't tell you I was coming through?"

"No. He didn't."

"Damn, well, yeah. Oh, this is my brother, Blaze," I said as I turned back to look at Blaze.

"Hey," he told the man and then put a bullet in between his eyes.

We both stepped over him and crept into the yacht. I knew there were security cameras everywhere, but I didn't care. I looked down and saw two packed suitcases by the entrance and shook my head.

"This nigga is gon' run," I whispered to Blaze.

Blaze followed me downstairs, and I saw Alastair sitting behind his glass bar, having a nightcap all by himself.

"Law, Blaze, to what do I owe the pleasure of this late visit?" he asked as he sat and sipped his drink.

"I saw your bags packed by the entrance. I thought you said you weren't leaving just yet," I said.

Instead of responding, Alastair simply nodded, pulled out his gun, and sat it on top of the bar.

"And I saw what you did to Ruiz at the door. He was one of my best men, you know? What was that about?"

"He was in the way." Blaze shrugged.

"I see." Alistair nodded. "Can I offer you two something to drink?"

"Nah," I said, shaking my head. "We good."

"Ah, no pleasure? That must mean you're here to talk business. Was there something wrong with your shipment?"

"Nah. Everything was straight," Blaze told him.

"Then why are you really here? I know you two didn't just come to have bullshit small talk."

"I want to know the real reason you're leaving Miami," I said.

I watched him tilt his head back and toss the rest of the dark liquor down his throat and then focus his attention back on me.

"Law, you know that in this game, you wake up every day to either gain a lot or lose a lot. It's always one or the other—never both. It's a mothafucking shame, but I love it."

"Don't say you love this shit if you ain't willin' to die for it," I said as I aimed my gun at him before he had a chance to pick his up.

"What the fuck do you think you're doing?" he asked as he raised his hands up.

His voice was calm, like he knew exactly what was about to go down. I saw his eyes quickly dart down to his gun, so I cocked mine.

"Don't try anything stupid, mothafucka. Blaze, take his gun."

After Blaze went over to take his gun, I continued talking.

"The bullshit you told me the last time we spoke ain't adding up, and I came here for the truth."

"I already told you the truth."

"Don't play with me. I'm not here for the fucking games."

"Killing me will start a full out war. Are you ready for that? Is that what the fuck you really want?"

"I just want to know why you're running, Al."

"You want the truth? Here's the truth! I could see the heat radiating off your ass from a mile away. You're young, Law. You're young, and you're fucking dumb! You little mothafuckas see your first few million from this shit and think you've made it. The key to this business is longevity."

"I am in this shit for the long run, nigga. Fuck is you sayin'?" I asked.

"You sound just like your father, and you know what happened to him."

"Don't you ever bring up our fucking father, nigga. You wish you were half the man he was!" Blaze interjected and pointed his gun at Alastair as well.

Alastair glanced at him and then turned his attention back to me.

"I'm disappointed, Law. You could've played your hand better. You just don't know how much shit you're into until you're knee deep in it, you stupid mothafucka. The cops want you, and they aren't gon' stop until they get you! Then what? They're gonna ask for your connect. And what are you going to tell them, huh? I'm not having any dots connected to me."

"Fuck the police. They gon' have to fight like hell to get me if they want me this time, nigga. No more fucking freebies. And what the fuck are you talkin' about? I was never selfish with my money, nigga. If I had food, everybody around me ate off that plate, including you, so what is you sayin', Al?"

"Look, Law. Shit is just too hot for me right now. I've spent too many years trying to keep my hands clean for the four of you mothafuckas to mess it up now."

"I can't just let you leave, Al. I thought I could trust you. My mother trusted you. My father fucking trusted you, but I don't like how you're moving right now," I said as I stepped closer to him and wrapped my finger around the trigger.

Alastair shook his head and then leaned his forehead against the tip of my gun.

"Do it, mothafucka. You got the balls to pull that trigger, then do it. I'd rather lay six feet under and comfortable than spend the rest of my life in a fucking box!"

My nostrils flared as I gripped the gun tighter and pulled the trigger twice. Glass shattered everywhere as Alastair's body flew backwards into his large liquor supply. His brain matter splattered all over his glass bar, the floor, and my clothes.

"Damn, nigga. That shit was cold blooded," Blaze said as he stared at Alastair's dead body.

"It is what it is." I shrugged.

"When are we going to tell those mothafucking Price boys the news?" he asked.

"In person. If they wanna eat, they gon' have to go through me now, and they better know it's never safe to bite the hand that feeds them."

"Oooh wee! Shit is about to be lit. I can't wait to see the look on their faces! They already mad as fuck!"

"Nah, I don't think those niggas mad enough. C'mon. Grab the shell casings, and let's get the fuck outta here."

I walked over and took Alastair's phone. Then Blaze and I picked up the two shell casings from my gun and the one from his outside and tossed them into the ocean. We left Alastair's yacht as quickly as we'd came. That was the thing about life. Everybody had plans. That fucking Detective Mason had plans. I knew those Price niggas and Shiya had plans, and so did I. Everybody was scheming in one way or another. My father taught me many lessons, but there was one that always stuck with me in particular. He told me to always do my dirt by myself. That way, there wouldn't be anybody around to tell on me if shit ever hit the fan. What Blaze didn't know was killing Alastair was just the first phase of my plan. I was going to turn all their plans on themselves and send their entire worlds crashing down one by one—even if it killed me.

CHAPTER SEVEN
Blaze

I was laying up, smoking a Cuban cigar, counting my money when my phone vibrated. It was Heaven. I got excited as shit when I saw her name pop up on my screen. I was hoping she was gonna come over and give a nigga some top while I smoked. That would've been love.

"Hello?" I answered.

"Hey."

"What's up?"

"I was wondering if I could come over to see you."

"You know what's funny? I was thinking the exact same thing when I saw your name pop up on my phone."

"Oh, yeah?"

"Yeah. You need me to come scoop you or you good?"

"Nah, just send me the address, and I'll drive over."

"Bet. I'm sending it to you now."

I hung up the phone, sent her the text with my address in it, and went to the bathroom to take a quick shower. Once I got out, I saw a message from Heaven saying she was ten minutes away.

"Bet," I said aloud.

I went downstairs to fix me a quick drink when my phone vibrated in my pocket. I put the bottle down and pulled it out.

"Hello?" I answered.

"Hey, I'm outside. I can park anywhere in this big ass drive-way?" she asked.

I chuckled.

"Yeah. I'm coming to the door now."

I hung up and shuffled over to the front door to unlock it for Heaven. I watched her get out of a navy blue 2009 Honda Accord.

"What's up. How you doin'?" I asked as I leaned down to hug her.

"Hey. What's up?"

"Shit, I was just in the kitchen fixin' me a drink. You want one?"

"Nah. I'm good," she said, holding her hand up.

"Okay then."

Heaven followed me into the kitchen, and I continued to pour my drink. Just by looking at her, I could tell she was being standoffish.

"Yo, you good?"

"I could be better." She sighed.

"What you mean? What's wrong?"

"Can we go somewhere private to talk?"

"Ain't nobody here right now but us. What's up?"

"Blaze, my period is late ..."

"How late?" I asked calmly.

"Like five days ..."

"You ever been late before?"

"Not like this," she said, shaking her head.

"Well, don't stress it. It'll probably come on like tomorrow or something." I shrugged.

"Yeah, but I already took a test."

"A pregnancy test? Don't you think that's jumping to conclusions?" I asked.

"Yeah, I just took it to get the thought out of my mind, but it was positive."

"Hold up. What?"

"Yeah ..."

"And you're just now telling me?"

"Blaze, calm down. I just took the shit like last night."

"Still, Heaven. It's a new day. Why you ain't hit my line before all that?"

"I just didn't wanna stress you if it wasn't nothin' for you to be worried about."

"And now you sittin' here tellin' me it's something."

"Yeah, I guess I am." She nodded.

I shook my head at her and took a big gulp of my drink. It burned going down, but I needed the alcoholic relief.

"So what you gon' do about it?"

"I don't know. I mean, like I told you the night I met you, I'm trying to finish school."

"Yeah, I think I remember you saying something about that, and I got shit to do out here, so it sounds like we both on the same page, right?"

"I mean, I don't know. I haven't made up my mind yet."

"What the fuck is that supposed to mean? You just sat here a second ago and told me you were trying to finish school. Now you don't know what decision you gon' make? What? You too scared to say the word? I'll say it for you, Heaven. Abortion!"

"Blaze ..."

"Nah, fuck that. You think it's that easy, huh? To have a baby with somebody you just fucking met? You don't even know my real name, and you would really consider havin' a fucking baby with me? Wake the fuck up, Nevaeh. Life don't work like that! There's no love story or trip to the bank in the midst of this shit! Fuck kinda schemin' ass shit is you really on?" I asked.

"Who the fuck you think you talkin' to like that? Like I ain't know what was up from the jump. You know how many niggas run through my job with money like you? Real, legit money? These niggas got more to offer me than just a few racks and a blinging ass necklace. They got real long money with dicks to match! Despite what the fuck you think, I didn't plan this shit! I'm just trying to be woman enough to let you know what the fuck is up! It's my body, and it's gon' be my decision whether I decide to keep it or not, but thank you for letting me know where the fuck you stand!" she yelled as she gritted her teeth at me.

"Yeah, okay. You talkin' 'bout you ain't plan this shit. Why the fuck you wasn't on no type of birth control anyway? No pill, no patch, none of that shit? C'mon now, Heaven. You should've been on some shit, especially with the shit you do for a living."

"I'm not a fucking prostitute! I don't fuck every nigga that walk through the doors of the club, nigga!"

"You could've fooled me!" I scoffed.

"What the fuck is that supposed to mean?"

"You know what the fuck it means. I came in there and brought you home to fuck on the first night. You mean to tell me you've never done that shit before?"

"If you thought I was such a fucking whore, then why the fuck you fuck me raw? Huh, nigga? You not gon' stand here and try to play me like I did this shit on my own!"

"Man, fuck you, bitch. I already told you what the fuck you need to do. You need money? Huh? Here!" I yelled as I pulled my wallet out my back pocket and tossed five one hundred-dollar bills at her. "Ain't that what you used to? Huh? That's probably not even my fucking baby, bitch. Get the fuck out of my house!"

Heaven stared down at the money as it trickled down to the kitchen floor and then looked back up at me, shaking her head.

"You know what? Fuck you, Blaze! You ain't nothin' but a wanna be boss ass nigga livin' in another nigga's shadow! Callin' me a bitch? Nigga, you the bitch! Grow up, and get your own fucking spot! How about that!" she yelled and stormed out of the kitchen and then out of the house, leaving the front door wide open.

I slammed the door behind her and marched right into the kitchen to pour me another stiff drink. Instead of pouring some more Henny into the glass, I just took the bottle straight to the head.

"Fucking bitch!" I yelled.

I didn't feel bad for dogging her ass out. I still couldn't believe the bomb she tried to drop on me like I was just gonna be cool with it. Yeah, the pussy was good, but she was fucking up my life with all that other shit. I wasn't ready to be a father, especially having a baby by a stripper. Heaven seemed like a cool girl, but I just couldn't get over the feeling that I was being played for a fool.

* * *

Raquel

Law and I were headed back to the house after grabbing something to eat. He slowed down when he pulled up to the house and saw a car neither of us recognized.

"Who the fuck is here?" he asked.

"I don't know. I've never seen that car before."

"Wait here," he said as he parked the car, grabbed his gun from the glove compartment, and got out of the car.

I watched as Law walked up to the car and knocked on the window. Instead of sitting and waiting, I got out of the car and followed him.

"Who the fuck are you?" he asked the person sitting in the car.

Law looked back at me and shook his head.

"I told you to wait in the car."

"What's going on?" I asked.

He walked over to me and started whispering.

"I don't know who that is, but she's sitting in the car fucking crying and shit. I don't know what the fuck she's saying. Probably one of Blaze's bitches. I hate when he be lettin' just anybody come over here."

"Let me talk to her and see what's up. You go find out if your brother knows her or not."

"Okay."

"Did you get her name at least?" I asked.

"Nah. I'll be back out in a minute. Be careful," he told me.

I nodded and walked up to the car and knocked on the window.

"Hey..."

The girl looked at me with tears in her eyes. There were black streaks of mascara stained on her cheeks, and I immediately felt bad for her.

"Are you okay?"

"I'm fine," she said, shaking her head.

"Are you waiting for Blaze to come outside or something?"

"Fuck that nigga." She sniffed.

"Oh... well... um... What's going on? Like, what are you doing here if you don't mind me asking?"

"I'm sorry. We just had a—a disagreement. That's all. Don't worry about it. I'm about to leave. I'm just getting myself together."

"I've never heard him mention you before. Did you two just recently meet?"

"You could say that."

"Well, then you know Blaze is a hothead. He's a good guy, but yeah."

"A good guy, huh?" she scoffed. "I have yet to see that side of him."

"What happened between you two if you don't mind me asking?"

"I don't want to talk about it."

"Oh, okay. That's fine, too. But... you seem pretty broke up about something. I'm guessing it's something he did or something he may have said," I said, fishing for a clue.

"I guess." She shrugged and wiped her face with the back of her hand.

"If you're this upset, then maybe it's just time for you to chuck it up as a loss and move on from the situation." I shrugged while trying to be as genuine as possible.

"I can't. I wish I could, but it's just not that easy."

"Why not?" I asked.

"I don't even know you, so I shouldn't even be telling you this, but... I'm pregnant."

"Oh shit."

"Yeah, 'oh shit' is right." She sniffed.

"And it's... it's his?"

"Yup." She nodded.

"Oh shit," I said again as I leaned against her car.

"So I take it he didn't take the news so well?"

"Oh no, he took it perfectly. I'm so happy right now. That's why you see me out here lookin' a fucking mess, right?"

"I'm sorry," I said, shaking my head.

"No, I'm sorry. I didn't mean to bite your head off like that. I'm just all fucked up right now."

"What's your name?"

"Nevaeh, but he seems to feel the need to call me Heaven."

"Oh... okay. Well, it's nice to meet you, Nevaeh. I'm Raquel."

"Hi," she said, giving me a quick smile.

"I'll try to talk to him. You know... if you want. I'm not making any promises, though."

"You can if you want. As far as I'm concerned, I've got my answer, and I'm done talking."

"Okay. Give me your number. We should keep in touch or maybe hang out sometime if you need someone to talk to. If you don't, that's cool, too."

"You don't have no friends, do you?" she asked.

"Not really. The ones I do have don't live here."

"Okay." She nodded.

I handed her my phone, and she plugged her number in and handed it back to me through the car window.

"It's going to be okay," I told her.

"At least one of us believes that," she said. "I'll see you around, Raquel."

"Okay."

Nevaeh started her car and pulled off. After she got out of the driveway, I turned to walk back in the house. Law was standing at the door, watching me.

"Damn, you scared me," I said, grabbing my chest.

"What happened?"

"Nothing happened. We just talked."

"About what?" he asked.

"Girl stuff. They had a fight. That's all."

"Who is she?"

"Blaze's friend. Have you seen him?"

"He's upstairs."

"Did you say anything to him about her?"

"He said he didn't want to talk about it."

"Okay. Well, I'm going to go talk to him really quick."

"Didn't I just tell you he said he didn't wanna be bothered."

"Yeah, by *you*. He hasn't said that to me yet." I smiled and walked upstairs to Blaze's room.

"Hey, Blaze. It's me. Can we talk?" I asked as I knocked on his door.

"I'm not really in the mood to talk right now, Raquel."

"I know. I just ran into your friend, Nevaeh, outside."

"She's still out there?"

"No. She's gone now."

"Good."

I opened the door and peeked inside.

"You good?"

"No."

"You wanna talk about it? May do you some good."

"Nah," he said, shaking his head.

I walked in and leaned against his dresser.

"She seems nice."

"What's your point?"

"My point is maybe you two should try to fix whatever happened between y'all."

"Did she tell you anything?"

"Yeah."

"Man, fuck!" he yelled.

"Did you tell my brother?"

"No. I didn't."

"Good. I don't want him to know. I don't want anyone to fucking know."

"Okay. I won't tell him. Your secret is safe with me."

"Thanks." He nodded.

"No problem."

I turned to walk out of the room and then turned back around.

"You wanna know what I see when I look at you, Blaze?"

"What's that?"

"A guy with a good heart that's too scared to just be himself and open up to one female. You just think you're going to miss out on something, but that's not the case. There's nothing out here."

"I don't believe that shit. There's always new pussy to be conquered, Raquel."

"See? That's your problem right there. You're the type of guy that girls can spot from a mile away, and it's not always because of your wild ass personality. You know what they say? The loudest nigga in the room is usually the most broke."

"I ain't broke. You know that."

"I know. I know that, but the point I'm trying to make is you don't have to be so... so..."

"So what?" he asked, sounding defensive.

"Predictable."

"What?"

"I'm just saying... If you stop doing what you've always done and try something new, then you might see a different side of yourself you never knew existed."

"I appreciate whatever advice you were tryna give me just now, Raquel, but I'm good, okay? Don't worry about me."

"Okay." I nodded and closed his bedroom door behind me.

I could see Blaze's insecurities written all over his face. He was so predictable that I knew exactly what he was going to say even before he did. All I wanted was for Blaze to tame his wild side, take accountability for his actions, and grow up a little.

* * *

Nashiya

Dallas showed up unexpectedly to my hotel room. It was my first time seeing him in a few weeks. I was still shaken up after my last encounter with Law, but I was happy I made it out with my life. All I had been doing since that day was sitting back and devising a new plan, which included Dallas's help.

"Long time no see, Bird," he told me.

"I know."

"I see you still held up in this hotel, huh?"

"Yeah, for now. I just gotta figure out my next move."

"Always scheming," he said, shaking his head.

"What's up, though?"

"Same ol' shit. 'Bout to re-up on some product from my connect later. Other than that, shit has been business as usual."

"Have you heard from Raquel?" I asked.

"Nah, not since before your wedding. Speaking of wedding, I heard through the grapevine that Law asked her to marry him."

I swallowed hard to try and keep my face emotionless, but on the inside I was falling apart piece by piece.

"Oh wow," I said.

"How you feel about that shit? You good?"

"Me? Yeah, I'm good. I guess it's true what they say. Bad news travels fast, huh?"

"Bad news for who?" he asked.

"Them." I smirked.

Dallas smiled, walked over, and kissed me on the forehead.

"You a ruthless ass bitch, you know that?"

"So I've been told."

"I gotta head up outta here though. I just came by to check on you. Don't worry about nothing, though. Just like we got the first nigga, we'll get Law and Blaze, too."

"I know you will" I smiled.

Dallas turned to leave and I walked into the bathroom and locked the door behind me. I turned on the shower and went to sit on the toilet. No sooner than my ass hit the seat, tears started pouring out of my eyes. I knew I was a complicated ass bitch, but I really did love Law. I might've had a fucked-up way of showing it, but it's not like anyone had given me a crash course on how to love somebody the right way. All I ever learned was how to steal and scheme.

I grew up a real hood girl. I mean, big bamboo earrings, Jordan's on my feet, all that. By hanging around my older sister, I learned real early how to switch my little hips to make it look like I had a big booty when I didn't. With that type of knowledge, I talked and walked my way right out of the hood and never looked back. I had older niggas tryna holla at me when I was only thirteen. I would always tell them no, but I couldn't lie—I loved all the attention. Nobody told me back then that all attention wasn't good attention.

Mother was a booster, so me and my older sister, Shayla, got the stealing shit honest. Neither one of our fathers were ever around. Mom said mine was a fly by night type of nigga. Whatever that meant. Shayla's was married and didn't want to leave his wife. There weren't too many girls around my way with daddies anyway, unless they were sugar daddies, so I didn't really feel like I was missing out on anything. By the time I was fifteen, my sister and I were shipped off to live with our aunt in Tallahassee because our mom got caught stealing and had to do almost two years in jail. Those were the worst two years of my life. My aunt had three sons, Demario, Jaquez, and Lamarcus, all at the age where all they cared about were the three F's—food, fighting and fucking.

Demario was the oldest. He was eighteen back then and a bona fide hustler. He was getting serious money, and although my aunt hated what he did, she loved seeing the consistent flow of income coming into the house, especially with two extra mouths to feed. He taught me and Shayla a lot about the game. Since she was two years older than I was, he didn't try to talk to her as much because she was too busy chasing dick. So, he spent a lot of his spare time with me, teaching me about scamming and stealing and even a little bit about the drug game.

"You got a cute face and shit, Nashiya. Anybody ever told you that before?" he asked me.

"Some of the boys at school, but I don't be paying them no mind."

"Why not?"

"You know all these young boys only be thinkin' about fucking."

"And you don't think about that?" he asked.

"I think about it. Just not all the time like they do."

"When you think about it, what do you be thinkin' about?"

"I don't know... maybe like the feeling or something."

"So then you are still a virgin, right?"

"Yeah. I am. What about it?"

"What's the most you've done with a boy?"

"Why are you asking me all this, Demario?"

"Because I wanna know."

"Just kissed. Let 'em feel on my titties, and I got fingered before."

"How'd it feel?"

"It felt okay."

"Just okay?" he asked.

"Yeah. I don't know how else to describe it."

"All that shit is supposed to feel good."

"Oh." I shrugged.

Demario walked over to me and grazed his hand against my cheek.

"I could show you if you want."

"You're my cousin," I told him.

"So, that's why you should trust me. I won't hurt you. I just wanna show you what pleasure feels like," he said as he backed me up into the corner of his room.

"Demario, no!"

"Lower your fucking voice before I crack your fucking skull, Shiya. I'm not fucking playin' with you!" he said through gritted teeth.

I stood silently in the corner as Demario started touching all over my body slowly. My legs were trembling as tears started rolling down my eyes. I knew everything that was happening to me was wrong and shouldn't have been happening, but truth was, I was scared of him. I knew the entire household depended on him to bring money into the house, and I didn't want to be the one to make him leave and have all of us sitting outside.

"Take your pants off," he said as he looked down at me.

I wiped my face with the back of my hand and started unbuckling my jeans. I shimmied them over my hips and left them around my ankles. Demario slid my cotton panties to the side and slowly inserted his finger inside me. I whimpered. It didn't feel good when he did it either. He slid his finger out of me after a few minutes when he didn't hear me making any noise and pointed to the bed.

"Lay down," he said as he walked over and locked his bedroom door.

I stepped out of my jeans and did as I was told. I watched Demario stand over me on the side of the bed, stroking his dick inside his pants. I quickly turned away and closed my eyes. Before I knew it, I felt my panties sliding down and Demario spreading my legs.

"I'm about to show you what real pleasure is," he told me as he kissed me. A few seconds later, he put his dick inside me.

Demario took my virginity that night and fucked me dozens of times over the two years I had to stay with him, my aunt, and his other brothers. I never told a soul what he did to me. The best thing about having Demario around was the money. He was always giving me money for school clothes or anything else I wanted just to make sure I kept our secret and he could keep fucking me whenever he wanted. Even though I was so fucked up in the head after that, I learned to never underestimate the power of the pussy. I didn't start dating Dallas until my senior year of high school. I was working a dead-end job, making fucking scraps. I didn't know shit about saving back then. He was nice, and most importantly, he wasn't family. He was just as broke as me, though, but I thought he was fine, so I stuck with him. I made him wait a long ass time to fuck, but once we started, we couldn't stop.

It wasn't until after we graduated and he really got into the drug game heavy with his brothers that he started really making money and feeling himself. All that shit messed things up between us. Once I realized I couldn't fight the world, and more importantly, I wouldn't fight the world for his time and attention, we broke up. I always figured the reason it was so easy for me to get Dallas to do my dirty work was because he felt bad about the way things ended between us all those years ago. If that truly was the case, I was going to milk that cow until it went dry.

CHAPTER EIGHT

Raquel

"Get dressed. We have dinner reservations in an hour," Law told me.

"What's the occasion?"

"I'm hungry." He chuckled.

"Wow. Really? And here I was thinking you were trying to be romantic. I should've known better."

"Damn, girl. You tryna eat or not?"

"I'm gonna go. Just give me a minute to hop in the shower and pick out something to wear," I told him.

"That's fine."

I walked into the bathroom, showered, and started fixing my hair. After that, I went and pulled out a strappy black dress and put it on.

"How do I look?" I asked as I turned to look at Law, who was sitting at the foot of the bed.

"You look beautiful."

"You promise?"

"Why would I lie to you?"

"I'm just checking." I smiled and walked back into the bathroom.

Law came and stood behind me as I applied my eyeliner and mascara in the bathroom mirror.

"Damn, girl. You look good from your lips all the way up to those crafty ass eyebrows of yours," he joked.

"Shut up!"

"I'm just saying! You look good. But now I know your secret, so don't let me go out and tell the world you fill in your eyebrows." He laughed.

"Oh my God! I hate you!" I laughed as I turned around and punched him in the chest.

"Are you almost ready?"

"Yeah, give me like three minutes and fifty-two more seconds, and I'll meet you down at the car."

"So precise." He laughed and then walked out of the bathroom.

When Law and I pulled up to the restaurant, I was in awe. The place was beautiful. We got out of the car, and I took in all the beauty around me that the place had to offer. There was smooth jazz playing in the background, and we had a beautiful view of the ocean as well as all of Miami. The city was beautiful at night with all the twinkling lights.

"This place is everything! Have you been here before?" I asked him.

"Once. It's not really my scene, but I wanted to take you somewhere nice."

"Is that why you look so uncomfortable?"

"Nah. I'm not. I'm just focused on you. I wanna make sure you have a good time."

"Anytime I'm with you is a good time, Law."

I watched him smile at me. He pulled his phone out of his pocket and put it face down on the table and grabbed my hand.

"So, is this the type of shit you're used to? You know? When you be datin' your lil' preppy college niggas and shit?"

"No," I said, shaking my head. "I don't think I've ever been to anything this fancy before."

"Well, I'm glad I could be your first."

"Yeah, you uh... turned out to be a lot of firsts for me, huh?" I joked.

"Very true."

Law and I stared at each other in silence, taking in everything about one another. It was a peaceful moment.

"What?" I smiled as I looked away, feeling shy.

"Nothing."

"No, say it."

"I'm just glad you're here with me tonight, Raquel."

Before I could respond, his phone vibrated. He picked it up and looked at the screen, sent a message, and then put his phone back down on the table.

"Is everything okay?"

"Yeah. Everything is fine. Don't worry about it."

I nodded and turned my attention to our waiter who had made his way over to us.

"Hello. What can I get you two to drink this evening?"

"Champagne for the lady and a glass of Hennessy on the rocks for me, please," Law said.

"Right away, sir."

I smiled when the waiter walked away. Law had more couth than he even knew. He kept showing me time and time again how perfect he was for me. After we got our drinks, we ordered our dinner, ate, and spent the next hour just taking in the scenery and enjoying each other's company. I noticed he kept looking at me strange all night, and every time I would ask, he would always brush it off.

"Are you sure you're good?" I asked.

"Yeah. Why you keep asking me that?"

"You keep looking at me funny. That's all."

"How am I looking at you?"

"Like you wanna say something, but you're not."

"I'm just trying to figure out the best way to give you this," he said as he reached in his pocket and put a box on the table in front of me.

"What is it?" I asked.

"Open it and see."

I took the box in my hand and slowly lifted the lid. Instead of looking down and seeing an engagement ring, I saw a car key.

"Law, what is this?"

"It's the key to your new car."

"What is this? A game show or something?" I chuckled.

"Nah. Nothing like that." He chuckled.

"Well, where is it? Let's go see it!"

Law put three $100 bills on the table, and we headed toward the parking lot. When I walked outside, I pressed the button and saw the car light up. It was a brand new, cherry-red Mercedes Benz.

"Oh my God, Law!" I squealed as I ran over to it and hopped behind the driver's seat.

It had woodgrain on the interior and chocolate-brown leather seats. I was in love.

"Is that all you see?"

"What else?" I asked as I looked up at him.

Law focused his eyes inside the car and I turned my head to look. There, hanging around the rearview mirror, was a chain with an engagement ring hanging on it.

"Oh my God," I said, putting my hands over my mouth.

"Grab it."

I carefully slid the chain from around the rearview mirror and held it in my hand. Law took it from me and looked me in my eyes.

"I'm not tryna be sappy, but I just wanna let you know that I listened to what you were saying before, and you were right. I didn't ask you to marry me properly, even during the sex, you know? So, I'm asking you right now. Even if your answer is still no, I want to spend the rest of my life with you in whatever way you'll let me. So, Raquel Valentine, will you marry me?"

"Yes, baby. I will," I said as I kissed him and wrapped my arms around his neck.

Law slid the ring on my finger, and I smiled.

"It's beautiful, baby. I love it."

"You deserve it. It was my mother's ring."

"It really is a beautiful ring." I nodded. "Thank you. I love you."

"I love you, too, Raquel."

I had finally gotten Law to tell me the three words my heart had been bleeding to hear ever since I told him how I felt inside the church. On top of that, I'd gotten the proposal I'd been dreaming of, and it wasn't a large production with a flash mob or a string quartet. It was me and the man I loved, standing in a parking lot next to my brand-new car. Everything was perfect until his phone rang. He pulled it out of his pocket and looked at the screen.

"Let me get this real quick."

"It's fine."

Law stepped away to take his phone call while I admired the ring he'd put on my finger and the new car that was all mine. The ring had a gold band and a large oval diamond in the middle. It was simple but still elegant. I was happy to be able to come and go as I pleased in my own ride without having to ask to borrow a car or ride with someone else. A few minutes later, Law came back with his head down.

"Is everything okay?" I asked.

"It will be once I go handle some things," he said.

"Things like what? You know what? Never mind. I don't want to know," I said, throwing up my hand.

I didn't want anything that could've possibly flown out of his mouth to ruin my night.

"Are you going to be alright if I leave?" he asked.

"Yeah. I'll be fine." I nodded.

"Are you sure?"

"Yeah. Just go handle whatever it is you gotta handle. I'll go home, and I'll be there when you get back."

Law sighed and kissed my forehead and then my ring finger.

"I'll see you back at the house, okay? I promise."

* * *

Law

I hated leaving Raquel like that, but Blaze and I had business to handle. I met Blaze down at the warehouse where Alastair pushed his weight through, pulled my duffel bag out of my trunk, and changed. I stripped out of my cufflinks, button up, and slacks and put on a black hoodie, black jeans, and matching Timbs. I grabbed my black gloves and shoved my pistol in the back of my pants. It was time to go to work. I pulled Alastair's cell phone out of the bottom of my duffel bag and texted Dallas's phone. Him and his brother, Darius, were coming to drop some money off and collect their new shipment in a matter of minutes. I knew their skin was going to turn pale as soon as they saw me there instead of Alastair.

"It's show time," Blaze said as he saw headlights flash toward the warehouse.

Blaze stood beside me as the Price brothers walked in with two duffel bags thrown over their shoulders. They both froze in their steps when they saw us.

"Law? Fuck is you doin' here?" Dallas asked.

"Sit down," I told him.

"Nah. Fuck that. Where the fuck is Al? I got his message."

"Sit down," I said again.

"Nah. Tell me where Al is."

"The nigga is dead! Now, sit down before I make you niggas sit down, nigga," Blaze interjected.

Dallas sucked his teeth. "Fuck outta here. I'm not fucking with you niggas."

"We about to let y'all niggas know how shit is gonna go down moving forward, aight? From here on out, I'm the plug. You want your product, you go through me," I told them.

"You motherfuckers can't be serious," Darius said, shaking his head.

"You thought we'd let you niggas just have this shit? You thought Miami was yours, nigga?" Blaze asked.

"You niggas done lost y'all minds," Dallas added. "I'm not fucking with you or you."

He pointed at both Blaze and I and then grabbed his pistol and aimed it at my forehead. I glanced over at Blaze, who was clutching his pistol tightly, itching to pull the trigger.

"Nigga, is you dumb or what? You can't just run up on us like that. I dare one of you niggas to touch me or my fucking brother!" Blaze told him.

"Look. You can pull that trigger, and it all ends here for all of us. No product. No money. No nothin'. Or, you can use your fucking brain, sit the fuck down, and continue to eat like the rest of us," I told Dallas.

I knew my words had put Dallas in between a rock and a hard place. The last thing he wanted to do was do business with us, but he knew just as well as I did if he wanted to continue to make money, he didn't have a choice. The drug business was nothing but a pyramid scheme in my eyes, and we had gone from being equals to him depending on me to eat in the blink of an eye. He shook his head, lowered his gun, and him and his brother sat across from me.

"That's a good boy." Blaze chuckled.

"Yo, Law, tell your baby bro to chill out with all the slick talkin' and keep his fucking mouth shut, nigga, before I crush his head into cake batter," Darius warned.

"Yeah, nigga. We ain't really into all the games you niggas are playing," Dallas added. "If you wanna do business, then do business."

"Nigga, who the fuck is playing games? I been the same mothafucka since I was in diapers, nigga. Fuck you talkin' about," Blaze said, popping off.

"Where's the money?" I interrupted.

"I got the money, nigga," Dallas assured me.

"Then put the shit on the table, nigga. We ain't got all night."

"Fuck you! If I said I got the money, then I got the money," Dallas said as he reached down to grab a duffle bag and put it on the table.

I stood up to unzip it and saw bands of cash.

"How much is this?"

"A hundred thou collected from my trap houses all over the 305," Dallas boasted.

"How much you want?"

"Ten kilos," he told me.

I nodded and gave him what he asked for. Darius put the product in his empty duffel bag and looked me up and down.

"Nice doin' business with you niggas," I told them.

I was ready to take both of those niggas out one by one until there wasn't anyone left, but I knew there was a time and a place for that shit. I wanted the world. Those niggas could have the trap as far as I was concerned. All I gave a fuck about was the money and puttin' those niggas in check. I knew they weren't going to continue to play fair, but that sale bought me some more time until the four of us had to cross each other's paths again. After Dallas and Darius left, Blaze turned to me.

"How you think that shit went? You think they gon' be cool?"

"I don't know. If they know what's good for them, they will. Niggas can't fuck with us. I been told you that."

"Right. We're not going anywhere, nigga. We right here," he paused. "Yo, Law. Can I holla at you about somethin' real quick?"

"What's up?" I asked, as I headed towards my car.

Blaze followed me out to my car and around the back to my trunk.

"You remember the bitch that was sitting outside in the car that night you and Raquel came home?"

"Yeah. What about her?"

"She called and asked if she could come over, right? I'm thinkin' cool. I'm about to tear that ass up real quick and send her back on her merry way. She comes over and she's actin' all funny, so I ask her what's up, and she tells me she's fucking pregnant."

"Hold up. What?" I asked, holding my hand out to stop him from talking.

"Yeah. That's what I said."

"Where'd you meet her?"

"Strip club."

"She was just there or she dance there?"

"Dance."

I clenched my jaw tight and shook my head.

"So what are you gonna do?"

"What can I do but continue to get to this paper?" he asked.

"I told you to be careful about what you were doin' out here in these streets, nigga. And with a stripper? What you think she in this for? For love? Ain't no way. She saw your flashy ass, and she saw dollar signs."

"I said all that to her, but she stay on some shit like it ain't like that. She don't even know if she wanna keep it."

"Of course, she wants to keep it so she can get money. Why strip when she got her own personal bank right here in you?" I said, shaking my head. "Damn, man! This is the last thing we need right now. I got this fucking court date coming up. We just got rid of one fucking gold digger, and now, you tellin' me we got another one on our hands? Fuck!"

"I know. You know how I am with these bitches, though. I just can't leave the pussy alone."

"Yeah, and now look where that shit got you. How do you even know it's yours? Did you strap up?"

"What you think?"

"Nigga, I don't know. Did you?"

"Nah... I didn't," he said, lowering his head.

"What the fuck!" I yelled and smacked him upside the back of his head. "I shouldn't be having to tell you none of this shit! You not a fucking kid no more, so why the fuck are you out here runnin' around like a horny ass sixteen-year-old boy?"

"I know I fucked up, but you should've seen her, Law. Plus, I was gone off the Henny and the loud. I just wasn't thinking straight."

"She's a fucking stripper, nigga! It's her job to look good. She said all the right shit, moved all the right ways, and everything, right? That's her fucking job! Now, she probably think because she sayin' she carrying your baby then you gotta be with her."

"You already know that shit ain't goin' down, nigga. I don't love these hoes," he said, shaking his head.

"You should've had that same mentality the night you fucked her. All these bitches want out here is to be saved and taken care of by niggas like us. They don't fuck with us for real, and you just handed her the key to the city in my eyes, no questions asked. All this money and pussy is gon' be the death of you, nigga!"

"Don't say that shit."

"I'm just being honest. Shit, you thought you was gon' tell me you had a baby on the way and I wasn't gon' speak my mind on it?"

"Well, it's too late now, nigga. What the fuck you want me to do?"

"She can't get an abortion?" I asked.

"That's what I said to her when she told me, but I don't know. She talkin' about some she don't know what she wanna do yet, and she hasn't made up her mind."

I shook my head.

"You gotta make better decisions, especially now that you might have a kid on the way. I ain't never had no baby, but I know it's a lot that comes with that parenting shit, Blaze. Are you ready for that? You see what Pops had to do to make sure we all ate, and you also see how that ended for him. You can't run in these streets like you been doing while you out here trying to raise a baby. These niggas will see your weakness from a mile away and use that shit against you."

"So what are you sayin'?"

"I'm saying that you need to make a decision. The streets or your kid because you can't have both."

Blaze sighed and shook his head.

"I just don't know, man. I don't know. What do you think I should do?"

"When's the last time you spoke to her?"

"That night you saw her car parked outside the house."

"You need to holla at her and see where her head is at. Once you find that out, you can make a decision. Just don't go into this shit blind, believing everything that comes outta this bitch mouth, man."

"You're right. I won't. I'm gonna talk to her again."

Blaze dapped me up and walked over to his car to pull off. I got back in my car, lit a blunt, and cracked the windows. I drove home thinking and smoking. I thought back to when I was young, barely a teenager, and couldn't run shit but my mouth. I had coke stashed in my dresser. In the middle of the night when everybody was sleep, I'd take it out and bag it up. Blaze caught me one night. I didn't want him to see me doing that shit, but I ain't really have a choice. I learned from Wolfe, and Blaze learned from me. After that, I vowed not only to protect my family but made sure I tried to set good examples if that was possible.

Blaze was far from stupid, but he was still in his early twenties and made impulsive ass moves that I either had to clean up or talk him out of. Unfortunately, his future lied in the hands of the bitch who claimed she was carrying his baby, and there was nothing I could do to save him.

CHAPTER NINE

Raquel

I woke up the next day to a text message from Camille.

Camille: Hey girl! My flight lands at 4:30 this afternoon. Pick me up from the airport. Toodles, bitch XOXO.

Raquel: I'll be there. Pinky promise me you'll have a safe flight, okay? XOXO.

Camille: Promise Pinkies.

I put the phone down and rolled over. Law wasn't lying beside me anymore. I slowly threw my legs over the side of the bed and rubbed the crust out of my eyes. It was time to get my day started because the last thing I needed was for Camille to be wandering around Miami waiting for me to come and pick her up.

I spent the rest of the day cleaning and making sure the guest room was nice and neat for Camille's stay. I had no idea how long she actually planned on staying, but I didn't mind the company and a familiar face. The rest of the day flew by, and before I knew it, I was on my way to the Miami International Airport to pick up my girl. As soon as we saw each other, we started screaming and ran to hug each other.

"Oh my God, bitch. It's been so long! Did you get taller?"

I laughed and pushed her off me.

"Shut up! I did miss your ass, though."

"I missed yours, too, girl," she said as she pinched my butt.

"You're so gay," I said, swatting her hand away.

"But um, hold up. Let me see the ring!"

I flashed her my ring, and she started screaming and jumping up and down.

"Oh my God, Raquel, it's beautiful. Like seriously, it's ten times better than that Cracker Jack ring Derrick gave you! No shade. I'm just saying."

"You ain't shit." I laughed. "But thank you. C'mon. Let's go."

I helped Camille with her bags and headed out toward my car.

"But really, Camille, how long are you staying? You've got enough luggage for six months, and this shit is heavy!" I groaned.

"I know, right? My bad, girl. You see the tag they put on it? Talkin' about some heavy luggage. Careful lifting." She laughed.

I pressed the keypad to unlock the trunk then drew back and lifted Camille's heavy ass suitcase up and flung it inside.

"Damn, is this your car, girl?"

"Yeah." I smiled. "He got it for me not too long ago."

"First, the ring, and now, the car? Oh, I'm liking Mr. Andreas more and more."

"I knew you would."

"So what's up, girl? What's really going on in the exciting world of Miss Raquel Valentine?" she asked as soon as I started the car.

I smiled and then sighed. I knew it was time that I came clean with Camille about everything that had transpired in my life since I'd last seen her. After all, she was my best friend. If I couldn't trust her, then who could I trust?

"I don't know where to start."

"Start from the beginning."

"So, the last night I saw you was crazy. I met Law after he saved my life."

"Wait. Saved your life how?"

"I got dragged into an alley, and I almost got raped by these two men. He found me, and he saved me by... you know."

"By what? Killing them?" she whispered as if we weren't the only two in the car.

"Yeah." I nodded.

I didn't feel the need to tell her the entire backstory on how Law and I really met. I did feel a little bad for lying, but I knew better than to tell her the entire truth... at least not right away. I wanted her to meet Law and get a real feel for him before judging him.

"So, what else happened? Y'all just hit it off just like that?"

"Not necessarily."

"What do you mean?"

"He had a fiancée when we first met. They didn't get married or anything like that. He broke it off with her. And now that we're together, I don't know. There's some days where I just can't help but feel like I'm living in her shadow, you know? Like before me, all he cared about was her, loving her, protecting her. Now, she's gone, and I'm just here asking myself is it real? Am I just a rebound?"

"But he loves you, right?"

"He says he does."

"He didn't give you her old ring, did he?"

"No. This was his mother's ring."

"Well, shit, that sounds like love to me. You know just as well as I do that you're a genuine ass, down-to-earth female, Raquel. Any man with sense isn't just going to let you slip through the cracks. Derrick did you a favor by showing you his true colors before your wedding just like his ex. If you ask me, it sounds like y'all just might be meant to be."

"You know... I never looked at it like that. You're probably right."

"Probably? I know I'm right! Well, I'll be able to see it when I meet him. You know I can read vibes from a mile away."

"I mean, yeah, okay. Well, let's just see what type of vibe you get when you get around him."

"Okay." She nodded.

"But hey, I've got a question."

"What's up?"

"When I didn't come home right after our Miami trip... did you go to the police?" I asked.

"No. I told you I thought about it, but I didn't."

"What about Shante?"

"I don't think so. Why? What's up? Is there something I need to know?" she asked.

"No. I just heard that she tried to file a missing person's report on me, and I was wondering if you knew anything about it."

"Oh, nah. I didn't. We had a little falling out when we got back from Miami anyway, so I haven't really talked to her."

"Oh God! Over what this time?" I asked.

"She was just being a bitch in Miami after you ditched us, and I told her ass about herself. She couldn't handle it, and she got mad. That's all."

"Oh... okay." I nodded.

When I pulled up to the house, Camille's eyes glazed over.

"Okay, first the car and now I see you livin' like this, bitch? Who is this nigga, and did God make any more of him for me?"

"He does have a brother."

"Jackpot! Where he at though? Is he fine? You know what? It don't even matter, bitch. As long as he got the ching, ching and some good ding, ding, I'm good."

"He a hoe, though. You don't want those problems."

"That's why God invented condoms, Raquel. Duh!" she laughed.

I laughed and shook my head.

"You're a trip," I said as I parked the car and got out.

Camille followed me into the house and into the kitchen. Law and Blaze were both standing in there talking.

"Hey, guys, this is my best friend, Camille. She's going to be staying here for ..."

"For a while," she said, extending her hand out to Law.

"Camille, this is Andreas, and this is Aston, his brother."

"Nice to meet you both," she said, focusing her attention on Blaze.

"Call me Blaze," he told her as he shook her hand.

"I'll be sure to remember that." She smiled.

Camille kept her eyes on Blaze until he left the room and then turned her attention back to Law and I.

"You ain't slick," I told her.

"What I do?" she asked.

"I saw the way you were looking at him."

"Girl, whatever. Anyway, Andreas, so you proposed to my girl and didn't get any permission from me? I got a problem with that."

"My bad, Camille. Do I have permission to make your best friend my wife?"

Camille looked him up and down for a second and then smiled and nodded.

"Yeah, you do."

"Okay, cool. Well, I'll let y'all get to doin' whatever it is y'all do," he told us and then kissed my forehead.

As soon as Law was out of earshot, Camille walked over and bumped her hip against mine.

"He definitely loves you, bitch."

"You can tell that quick?"

"Uh, duh. I told you I'm quick with it. Shit, everybody can probably see it, and they don't have to know either one of you. I've only been here for a hot second, and I can see it. It's not even what I see, it's what I feel when the two of you are in a room together. That shit is like... I don't know... like a magnetic force between y'all. It's kind of creepy."

"Why creepy?"

"All that time you were with Derrick, I never saw you like

that. Yeah, you loved him and all that, but girl, it's just not the same. You got a real one on your hands. That's all I'm saying."

"You're right about that." I nodded.

* * *

Blaze

A couple days later, I was chilling in my room when I heard a knock at my door. Truth be told, I didn't feel like being bothered, but I got up and answered it anyway. To my surprise, it was Raquel's friend, Camille.

"Hey... Blaze, right?" she asked.

"Yeah, what's up?"

"I know this is kind of random, but, um, can I use your shower?"

"What's wrong with Raquel's or the one in the guest room?"

"They are both occupied." She shrugged.

"You know there are like at least five other showers in this house, right?"

Camille stepped back and rested all her weight on her back leg, and then switched.

"Are you going to let me use yours or not?"

"Fine," I said as I pointed to the bathroom. "Right through that door."

"Thank you."

Camille walked into the bathroom and closed the door behind her. As soon as the door closed, I realized I had to use the bathroom.

"Shit, man," I groaned.

After a few minutes, I heard the shower turn on, so I walked inside. Camille was standing there with the shower curtain pulled back with soap all over her body.

"Hey." She smiled.

"Hey," I said. "I just had to take a piss real quick. I didn't think you'd be in here showering with the shit all open."

"You like what you see?" she asked as she turned around and started making her ass clap for me.

Soap and water were flying everywhere, and I watched her ass jiggle and her titties bounce. She didn't take her eyes off me as she washed herself. She started rubbing on her breast and pussy. I wanted to look away, but what can I say? A dog gon' be a dog.

"Come here," she told me.

"Camille..."

"Shh... they don't have to know."

I pulled my shirt over my head and then slid my basketball shorts and boxers down. I took my socks off and looked down. My dick was already standing at attention. I turned to lift up the toilet seat and piss, shook my dick, and then washed my hands. As soon as I turned the faucet off, I turned my attention straight back to Camille. She let the water run down the small of her back to wash away all the soap from her ass. She cuffed her hands underneath her ass to spread her cheeks apart and show me her pussy. I watched the water run down the opening of her hairless pussy and down the back of her thighs.

"Damn, girl. What are you tryna do?"

She reached out and grabbed my hand and put it on her wet ass.

"C'mon, Camille. You're Raquel's friend. I'm not tryna start nothing."

"You gon' make me fuck myself, Blaze?"

"Nah, I mean... I'm just saying."

"I told you. Nobody has to know. It'll be our little secret," she said as she leaned against my shower wall and spread her pussy lips wide open for me.

Camille started moaning and rubbing on her titties again. She reached out and grabbed my dick and started rubbing it then dropped down to her knees and started giving me head. Her mouth was warm and her jaws were tight.

"Mmm, shit," I groaned as she started deep throating my dick until she gagged.

"Come here," I told her, as I pulled her to her feet. I spun her ass around and grabbed a whole handful of her juicy ass then smacked it. I wasn't trying to slut her out, but she was asking for it.

"Mmm." She smiled.

"You a freak, you know that?"

"When I see something I want, I go after it. That's all. I'm not lookin' for nothin' else but a good time."

"That's exactly what I wanted to hear."

I slid my dick inside her and started fucking her with no mercy. Then I pulled out of her. Her pussy was tryna get a nigga caught up for a second time, and I couldn't have that shit.

"Come to the bed."

She shut the shower off and followed me to the room. I threw her wet, naked body on the bed, slid a condom on, and started fucking her from behind again. I grabbed both of her arms and held them behind her back while I fucked her so she couldn't try to run away from the dick.

"Mmm... shit... Your dick is big as fuck, Blaze."

"I know. Now, take that shit. You gon' take that shit?"

"Mmm... Yes... I'm gonna take it all."

I let go of her arms and pushed her head down into the pillow.

"Good. Now, stay down and take all this dick."

Camille reached around and spread her ass cheeks so that I

could go deeper into her pussy. She was moaning so loud I knew somebody was going to notice, so I reached around and put my hand over her mouth. I turned her around and started fucking her with my hand still over her mouth. She grabbed my hand and moved it down to her throat. She made sure it didn't leave her throat like her ass wanted to lose consciousness or something. She let out hoarse squeals of pleasure as I continued to fuck her.

"Don't run, Camille. This is what you said you wanted, right?"

I pulled my dick out and slapped it against her pussy then smacked her ass. I pulled the condom off and tossed it on the floor.

"Come suck my dick some more."

Camille crawled on all fours as I laid back, relaxing. She sucked my dick for a few minutes then stopped.

"Why you stop?" I asked her.

"I want more of this. Get another condom."

"You don't quit, do you?"

"Nah, I'm not done until I ride it."

I smiled and reached over into my nightstand to grab another condom and tossed it at her. Camille opened the wrapper, slid it on my dick, and then climbed on top of me. She started riding the shit out of my dick. I held her waist as she bounced up and down on my shit like her head was about to start spinning off her shoulders.

"Fuckkkkk yessssss, Blaze! I'm coming! I'm fucking coming!" she screamed.

"Get that fucking nut," I said as I smacked her ass.

I could feel myself about to nut, so I pushed her off me and slid the condom off. I jacked my dick off into her mouth and held the back of her head until I came. Camille licked her lips and swallowed my nut.

"Mmm... shit," I said.

"I knew that shit was gonna be good the moment I saw you,"

she said as she walked back into the bathroom and turned the shower back on.

I shook my head and patted myself on the back for being a lucky ass nigga. Once Camille left the room, I laid back against the bed and started thinking about Heaven. Even after talking to Law, I still hadn't reached out to her. I rolled over, grabbed my phone, and called her.

"Hello?"

As soon as I heard her voice, I started to realize how fucked up I was to her. It had me feeling bad. I knew that I'd overreacted and could've let a good girl slip through my fingers.

"Hey ..."

"What do you want?"

"Look, I just wanna talk, aight?"

"I think you've said enough, and I haven't heard from you in weeks."

"I know, and I wanna be the bigger man and apologize for that shit. I shouldn't have talked to you that way."

"Yeah, you're right. You shouldn't have."

"I was wondering if we could... you know... start over or something."

The phone went silent.

"Hello? You still there?"

"I'm still here."

"Did you hear what I said?"

"Yeah. I heard you," she said.

"So ..."

"Um, I don't know."

I sighed.

"Look, Heaven, I know I fucked up, but this is me trying to make shit right with you, and I ain't never done that before with no bitch. I mean... with no female, okay? We can just take it at your pace if you want."

"If I say no sex, you can handle that?" she asked.

"No sex!" I yelled.

She laughed.

"Yeah. That's what I said."

"Damn, man. I don't know."

"Well, that's where I stand. We need to seriously figure some things out before I ever let you hit this again."

"What about letting me taste it?" I smirked.

"You are so nasty!"

"You like it though."

"Yeah, I might."

"Can I see you?" I asked.

"When?"

"Shit, now. I can slide through to your place, or you can come here. You know what? Send me your address. I'm going to come scoop you. Is that okay?"

"Um, yeah. That's fine."

"Aight, bet." I smiled and hung up the phone.

I couldn't wipe the smile off my face if I tried. I felt good for trying to set things straight with Heaven and finally doing the right thing. I hopped in the shower, got dressed, and checked my phone to see if Heaven had sent me her address. She did.

"Bet," I mumbled and headed outside to my car.

I plugged her address into my GPS and went to pick her up. After about thirty minutes, I pulled up to an apartment complex and parked in the visitor's section then called her.

"Hello?"

"Yeah. I'm outside."

"Okay. I'll come down."

I hung up and sat outside waiting for Heaven to come out. When I saw her, I flashed my lights at her. She walked over to my car and got in.

"Hey."

"Hey," she said. "Did you have any trouble finding my apartment?"

"Nah. It was pretty easy. I actually remember coming around this area when I was younger."

"Oh, really?"

"Yeah. I used to run in the streets heavy back then."

"I bet."

The two of us sat in silence for a few seconds, and she turned her attention to whatever was going on outside of the passenger side window.

"Hey. Um... I've been thinking about all that baby shit, and I want you to do whatever you feel is right. If you wanna keep it, I'm down. If you don't, I'm down for that, too."

"I have been doing a lot of thinking on it," she said.

"And?"

"And I'm going to keep it, Blaze. I'm going to keep our baby."

"Oh... okay." I nodded slowly, trying hard not to show emotion.

"Okay? That's all you're going to say?"

"Yeah. I mean, shit. I guess we having a baby," I told her.

"Okay then." She nodded.

"This is going to be different. I don't know the first thing about raising a baby."

"Me either."

"And I don't even know where this puts you and I, but as long as you fucking with me, I'm fucking with you, Heaven."

"You know you gon' have to stop callin' me that, right?"

"That's your name, though."

"It's Nevaeh. Heaven spelled backwards."

"I'm still gonna call you Heaven until the day I die. No other nigga can call you that shit but me, aight?"

She smacked her lips, looked me up and down, and then smiled.

"Fine."

"But for real though... were you serious about that no sex shit?"

"I was kidding, Blaze."

"Good," I said as I ran my hand down her thigh. "Because you lookin' too damn good right now."

"Stop it," she said as she smacked my hand.

"What I do?"

"Your ass still ain't off the hook yet!"

I laughed at her and shook my head.

"You got it."

"So, you wanna come up for a little bit? My house ain't nothin' compared to yours, but it'll be just you and me."

"Yeah. That's cool."

"Just remember to keep your hands to yourself."

* * *

Law and I decided on a small, intimate wedding. I didn't want to wear an extravagant gown or have any of the traditional bells and whistles that all the typical weddings had. I just wanted it to be more about me and him and celebrating the love we had for each other that was growing by the day. Camille was sitting next to me in the living room talking about wedding stuff. I knew I wanted her to be in my wedding, but I also decided to reach out to Nevaeh. She seemed like a cool girl, and I wanted to see if she and Blaze had worked out their situation. I picked up my phone to text her.

Raquel: Hey, Nevaeh, it's me, Raquel.

Nevaeh: Hey. What's up?

Raquel: My friend is in town and I wanted to know if you wanted to come hang with us for a little bit if you're up to it.

Nevaeh: Yeah, sure, that's cool. Where?

Raquel: I was thinking we could all go out for dinner and drinks. Send me your address and I'll pick you up around 8.

Nevaeh: I'll go, but no drinks for me. We're keeping the baby.

"Oh shit," I said out loud as I stared at my phone.

"What's up?" Camille asked as she scooted closer to me on the couch.

I looked over my shoulder and then back at Camille.

"Okay, so I met this chick a few weeks ago. She was parked in the driveway, crying her eyes out. She told me that her and Blaze had a falling out or whatever."

"Is she his girl or something?"

"Nah. I mean, I don't think so. We had never heard him mention her at all before that night."

"Okay. Keep going."

"So, I'm trying to talk to her and see what's up. You know? Lend a listening ear. She tells me that she's fucking pregnant with Blaze's baby."

"Oh shit," Camille said.

"Exactly! So at first, he didn't want anybody to know about it, so I didn't say shit. But I just texted her, and she told me that they decided to keep the baby."

"Damn, that's wild," Camille said as she scooted back to the other end of the couch.

"I know, right? Can you imagine Blaze with a kid?"

"I don't know." She shrugged.

Camille turned her attention back to the TV, and I stared at her with my forehead scrunched up.

"What's wrong with you?"

"Huh? There's nothing wrong with me. Why would you ask that?"

"I'm just saying... Your body language changed after I just told you all that."

Camille rolled her eyes and then turned back to face me.

"So..."

"So what? What did you do?" I asked.

"I may have fucked your soon to be brother-in-law ..."

"Hold up. You did what?"

"Yeah. I don't know. It just kind of happened... I mean. What can I say? I like to fuck." She shrugged.

"I was gonna ask her to be in my damn ceremony! That shit is out the window now! Oh my God! I need all the details, and I mean the who, what, when, where, and most importantly, why!"

Before Camille could open her mouth, my phone rang.

"Hold that thought," I said as I looked down at the screen. "Fuck!"

"What? What is it?"

"It's Derrick. What do I do?"

"I don't know. Answer it? Decline? What do you want to do?"

"I don't know! I feel like if I don't answer, he's going to keep calling," I said.

"Well, pick it up then before he hangs up!"

"Fine!" I told her and pressed the accept button. "Hello?"

"Put it on speaker, bitch," Camille whispered.

I rolled my eyes and pressed the speaker button then put the phone down on the couch in between Camille and I.

"Hello?" I said into the speaker.

"Hey, Raquel. It's me, Derrick. I'm in Miami ..."

CHAPTER TEN

Ian

I was downtown with my lawyer, Clifton, at his office. He was talking to me about the case and preparing me for my court hearing in a few days.

"Andreas, I'm going to ask you this one last time. Is there anything that I need to know before you walk in front of that judge in a few days?"

"No," I said, shaking my head. "I didn't kill Damien."

"And you're sure that the D.A. won't be able to drill a hole in your story? I can't fully defend you if I don't know everything there is for me to know. I told you that."

"I know, and I'm telling you, Clifton, everything is on the up and up. I just need you to do your job and get rid of this case so I can get this fucking detective off my back."

"Speaking of the detective, his name was Shawn Mason, right?"

"Yeah. That's him. What about him?"

"Remember when you asked me to do some digging?"

"Yeah. What'd you find? Anything good?"

"Not really. He's a good one, and if he is dirty, he makes sure he keeps things clean around him."

"What about his family? Anybody close to him?"

"A deceased sister killed by a drunk driver when she was nineteen."

"Anything else?"

"Uh, well, I did find one piece of information that might be of some value to you."

"Okay. What is it?"

"There was a brother."

"Was or is?" I asked.

"Is. He's still alive, and it looks like he's in jail right now for the murder of a police officer. But wait," he said as he continued to type and scroll. "The officer was Mason's old partner. Right before he got killed, it looks like Mason was transferred to another precinct."

"Why?"

"It doesn't say. People get transferred for different reasons all the time, but the timing is what stands out to me the most. You just give me some more time, and I'll get the questions answered that you need."

"Thanks. Hey. Send me the link to that article or whatever it is you were looking at."

"I'm on it. Say no more. You just make sure you're ready to put your game face on in that courtroom when the time comes."

"I will be," I assured him.

As soon as I left Clifton's office, I hopped in my car and headed straight to my mother's house. I had been avoiding the thought of her being sick. I knew that with my court date coming up, I wanted to put all the cards out on the table and let her know that I knew what was really going on.

I loved my mother more than I loved any woman on this Earth. I remember when I first got with Nashiya. She saw how happy I was, and although I knew she didn't like her, she gave me her wedding ring from her marriage with my father anyway. She said out of all her sons, she knew I was going to be the one to settle down and do right by one woman. I thought Shiya was that woman, but for some reason, I couldn't bring myself to give her my mother's ring, so I went out and bought her one from the jewelry store. After everything that went down with Raquel and I, I was glad that I waited to give her that ring instead.

When I pulled up to my mother's house, I got out and knocked on the door.

"Who is it?" she asked.

"It's me—Andreas."

"What are you doing here?" she asked as she peeked around the door, making sure she didn't let me see all of her body.

"Blaze told me, Ma. You don't have to hide anymore."

My mother sighed and fully opened the door for me.

"I told his ass not to say shit to you. I wanted to be the one to tell you."

I walked past her and headed into the living room. She followed me and sat next to me on the couch.

"How are you feeling?" I asked as I pulled her into my arms.

"I have good days, and I have bad days."

"What's today?"

"So, so," she said, tilting her hand from side to side.

"I still don't understand why you didn't tell me about your situation. Why didn't you want me to know?" I asked.

"It wasn't that I didn't want you to know. It wasn't something I planned to hide from you forever, Andreas. I just... I don't know. You were marrying that tramp, and we weren't really speaking because I didn't want to come to your wedding. It was just a mess. I didn't think you could handle it. Plus, I didn't want that girl knowing my business."

"You don't have to worry about her anymore, Ma. She's out of the picture for good."

"Your brother told me. I'm proud of you," she said as she put her hand on top of mine.

"I do have somebody else that I'm seeing, though. Her name is Raquel. I know you'll like her."

"Raquel, huh? That's a pretty name, so she must be a pretty girl, right?"

"Yeah. She is."

My mother smiled and then leaned her head back against the couch.

"You alright?" I asked.

"I'm fine. Just feeling a little sick to my stomach. The medicine they've got me taking makes me queasy some days."

"Ma, the real reason I came here was to ask you to move into my guest house."

"Your guest house? For what? I'm perfectly fine right here in my own home, Andreas."

"I knew you were going to say that, but it would really make me feel at ease. I would make sure you had everything you needed, someone to take you back and forth to your doctor's appointments, make sure you take your medicine on time, around the clock care... anything you want."

"What I want is to stay here, in my own home. I don't need all of that."

"Yes, you do. I wish you would stop trying to be so strong all the time, and just let me take care of you like you took care of all of us."

"Strong is the only way I know how to be," she told me. "But if it really means that much to you, I'll do it on one condition."

"What's that?" I asked.

"You have to let me meet Raquel and feel her out for myself."

"Done."

CHAPTER ELEVEN

Raquel

After Derrick told me that he was in Miami, Camille convinced me to meet with him briefly. She told me I needed to show him my glow up status and make him regret ever cheating on me in the first place. I agreed and told him that I would meet him at a restaurant in Little Havana down in South Beach.

When I walked into the restaurant, I scanned the place and locked eyes on the back of Derrick's head. He was sitting at the bar. I walked up beside him and sat my purse down on the bar.

"Derrick."

He turned to look at me and smiled. My stomach did a slight backflip. It wasn't like he looked bad like I had wanted. He looked the same. He was wearing a black button up shirt with a gray and white striped tie, black slacks, and black dress shoes.

"Raquel," he said and stood up to hug me. "I'm so happy you could make it. To be honest, I didn't think you were going to show up."

"Well, to be honest, I didn't know if I was going to show up, either." I shrugged.

"So, what's new? How have you been?"

"Engaged," I told him.

"Wait. You're what?"

"Yeah."

"Wow. um... I don't know what to say, except for maybe that was fast."

"How long were you fucking Yasmine behind my back, Derrick?" I asked, cutting straight to the chase.

"Huh?"

"You heard me. Answer the question."

Derrick sighed and shook his head. He was a fool if he didn't think I wasn't going to bring that shit up the moment I saw him.

"Raquel, I ..."

"I don't want to hear any excuses, Derrick. Just tell the truth."

"It had been going on for about a little over a month or two when you saw what you saw."

"Say the words, Derrick. When I walked in on you fucking my roommate six months before our fucking wedding!" I yelled.

A tear stung my eye and then slid down my cheek.

"Please, don't cry, Raquel," Derrick said, reaching out to wipe my tear.

I quickly swatted his hand away.

"Don't touch me. I'm fine. I guess I just never really dealt with it until now," I admitted.

"I feel horrible. Probably even more now than I did then because I can see how much I hurt you. You know one of the main reasons I was so eager to get down here was because I wanted to see you. I wanted to tell you how sorry I am for all the things that I did to you. I wasn't good boyfriend material or good fiancé material. Whatever you wanna call it... and I'm sorry. I never should've put you through any of that, and now, it sounds like I've pushed you right into the arms of another guy."

"You're absolutely right. You shouldn't have. All I ever did was for you... for us. I was going to give myself to you, Derrick! I wanted you to be the only man for me, but you just couldn't hold out, huh? Did you fall in love with her?"

"No, I didn't. I loved you. I still love you, Raquel. I just don't know how to take it when you tell me that you're engaged to someone new. After all we've been through, don't you think you can try to give it one more shot with me? I swear to God everything is out of my system now, and I'm ready to be committed to you and only you, mind, body and soul for the rest of my life."

I shook my head as I stood to my feet.

"As much as I probably needed to hear you say those words, Derrick, there will never be a future for us. I've moved on, and I suggest you do the same. It's better that way for the both of us."

* * *

Nashiya

I was walking around in South Beach, trying to get my head on straight when I saw Raquel walk out of a restaurant across the street from me. Seconds later, I saw a tall, brown-skinned man chasing after her. They shared words, and although I couldn't hear exactly what they were saying, I could tell there was passion between them. Raquel jumped in her car and sped off, while the man stood there watching her drive away. After a few seconds, he turned around to walk back inside the restaurant.

I scurried across the street and walked into the restaurant and headed straight for the bar where he was sitting.

"What can I get you, ma'am?" the bartender asked me when I walked up and sat down beside the man.

"Uh, a shot of tequila and one of whatever he's having," I said, pointing to the man.

He turned to look at me.

"It's a screwdriver."

"Then I'll take one of those, and bring another one for my friend here," I said.

"Isn't the man supposed to be the one buying the drinks?" he asked me.

"Maybe today is just your lucky day." I smiled. "I'm Nashiya by the way."

"Nashiya, I'm Derrick, and thanks for the drink. I could really use one right about now."

"Yeah. I saw that little thing you had going on outside before I walked in."

"Damn, you saw that? That's embarrassing."

"Anything you wanna maybe talk about from one stranger to another?"

"Uh, I don't even know if there's that much to say, really. I came down here for a work event. That girl you saw was my ex-fiancée."

"Oh, wow. Really?" I asked.

"Yeah." He nodded.

"Why'd you two call the wedding off if you don't mind me asking?"

"I was a dumb ass. That's why."

"Hey, we've all been there. So, did you try to give it another go?"

"What you saw was my attempt at doing that, and she wasn't having it. She basically told me that she's moved on, and I should do the same. I ain't gon' lie. That shit stung a bit but not more than when she dropped the bomb on me and told me that she was engaged."

"Oh shit. I'm sorry to hear that," I said, patting him on the back.

"Yeah, that shit sucks, but I guess it's what I get. She deserves to be happy."

"And you don't think she can be happy with you, Derrick?"

"I told her I was ready to be committed and do right by her, but she wasn't trying to hear it, so I just left it alone."

"Do you love her?"

"Of course, I do. I always will." He nodded.

"Well, here's some unsolicited advice from, again, one stranger to another. If you love her, go after her."

"What do you mean? Like, stop the wedding?"

"You take it however you want to, but I'm a woman, and I know what women want. We want a man to profess his love for us in more than just words. We want actions behind it. Sounds to me like your ex is just playing hard to get, and this other guy is nothing but a rebound."

"Maybe you're right." He nodded.

"I'm telling you. What happens in all the good romantic movies? The girl leaves, the guy chases her, and they always end up being together in the end, right?"

"Yeah."

"I'm not saying your life is like a sappy love movie, but still, you get the picture."

"Yeah, you're right. If I love her, which I do, I need to put up more of a fight for her and show her."

"Precisely." I smiled.

"Thank you... Nashiya, right?"

"Yup. That's me."

"Thanks."

"No problem. I'm going to get out of here now, but you finish the rest of your drink and figure out a way to get your girl back. I'll be rooting for you."

I patted Derrick on the back once more, tossed my shot down my throat, and left some cash on the bar to cover my drinks and his, too. It was almost too hard to contain the smile that was growing across my face. Once again, I had put my slick ass tongue to good use. All I had to do was sit back and watch Raquel and

Law's relationship unravel layer by layer. It was going to be like taking candy from a baby.

* * *

Law

I woke up early on the morning of my court hearing feeling confident that I didn't have anything to worry about. Detective Mason had stopped pursuing Raquel, and I was thankful because we hadn't gotten the chance to get married before my court date came up. I put on a crisp, white button up, clean black slacks and a pair of black dress shoes. I walked over to Raquel, who was laying in the bed staring at me as I got dressed.

"Good morning," I told her.

"Good morning, baby. Today's the big day. How are you feeling?"

"I'm feeling pretty good. Are you sure you're okay with not coming to the courthouse?"

"Yeah. I mean, I think we both agreed that it was for the best just in case the D.A. tries to pull some last-minute shit. I don't want to be the reason they try to lock you up, especially for something you didn't do."

"Okay. I was just making sure." I nodded.

I walked over to her side of the bed and kissed her forehead.

"I'll see you after court."

"Okay." She nodded.

I left the house and headed down to Clifton's office. We went over everything that the D.A. would probably try to use as evidence against me, then we rode down to the courthouse together.

"You sure you're okay?" he asked before we walked into the courtroom.

"Yeah. I'm good." I nodded and pushed open the courtroom door.

"Remember, the key is to make sure the judge doesn't let this go to trial. We're going to work to get all of the charges against you dropped today, okay?"

"Okay." I nodded.

Once the judge walked in, we all stood until he was seated. The dumb ass detective was there, smiling like he knew he was going to put my ass under the jail. I sat down and adjusted my posture in my seat. The D.A. presented the evidence they had and then called Detective Mason to the stand.

"Detective Mason, do you swear to tell the truth, the whole truth, and nothing but the truth, so help you God, under pains and penalty of perjury in this court of law?" the bailiff asked.

"I do."

"Detective Mason, can you please tell us what you do for a living?" the D.A. asked.

"Yes. I work for the cold case unit for Miami PD."

"And what business did you have involving the Damien Price case?"

"I was assigned to look into the case and try to close it."

"And do you believe you've done that to the best of your abilities in this courtroom today?"

"Yes, I do."

"And why is that?"

"I believe Andreas Calloway killed Mr. Price in cold blood."

"Objection!" Clifton shouted out.

"Sustained. Carry on carefully, Mr. Mason," the judge told him.

"I'm sorry, Your Honor, but I've had the D.A. present evidence of the video footage from the hotel and the partial 911 call that was made by the female who witnessed the murder. Her name is Raquel Valentine. She also happens to be Mr. Calloway's newest love interest."

"Why do you think that is?" the D.A. asked. "Could it be because she knew something that could implicate him for this murder?"

"Objection!" Clifton shouted out again.

"I'm sorry, Your Honor."

"I believe that Andreas had that young woman kidnapped and has brainwashed the only victim to this heinous crime to believe that he is the good guy and he did not kill Mr. Damien Price, when in fact, he did!"

"Thank you, Mr. Mason. No further questions."

"Does the defense have any questions for Mr. Mason?" the judge asked.

"Yes," Clifton said as he stood up and buttoned his suit jacket.

"Mr. Mason, how long have you been in law enforcement?"

"Almost eleven years."

"And out of those eleven years, have you always upheld the law?"

"Yes. I took a sworn oath to serve and protect the people of the city of Miami, and I've done that every single day for the past eleven years."

"And have you always worked alone?"

"No. I used to have a partner, but he was killed in the line of duty."

"*Used to* is the key word here. Now tell me, Detective, was he killed before or after you were transferred to another precinct?"

"Objection, Your Honor, what does Detective Mason's career history have to do with any of this? He is not the one on trial here today," the D.A. said.

"Overruled. Keep going, Mr. Jones."

"Thank you, Your Honor. I promise you I'm going somewhere with this."

Clifton turned to look back at the detective.

"Could you please answer the question?"

"I was transferred before."

"And correct me if I'm wrong, Detective, but wasn't it your very own brother who was convicted of the murder of your partner?"

The detective swallowed hard and then nodded.

"That is correct."

"You see, Your Honor, can somebody tell me how anyone can expect a man to protect and serve when his own flesh and blood killed a member of our very own law enforcement community?"

"Objection, Your Honor!" the D.A. yelled out again.

"I think that you thought that pinning the murder of Damien Price on my client, an innocent man, would get you back in the good graces of your peers, isn't that right, Mr. Mason?"

"Objection!"

"Sustained!" the judge yelled out and smacked his gavel down. "That's enough, Mr. Jones."

Clifton nodded and walked back to our table.

"The defense rests, Your Honor. No further questions."

"Call your next witness," the judge said to the D.A.

"Prosecution calls Mr. Andreas Calloway to the stand at this time, Your Honor."

I stood up and walked to the stand to sit down. The bailiff walked over to me with a bible and told me to raise my right hand.

"Andreas Calloway, do you swear to tell the truth, the whole truth, and nothing but the truth, so help you God, under pains and penalty of perjury in this court of law?" the bailiff asked.

"Yes." I nodded.

"Mr. Calloway, where were you the night Mr. Damien Price was murdered?" the D.A. asked.

"I was at home with my then, fiancée, Nashiya," I said.

"The two of you haven't gotten married yet, correct?"

"We called the wedding off."

"And is it true that you are now in a relationship with the witness, Miss Raquel Valentine?"

"I am."

"And when did the two of you meet?"

"A few months ago."

"Around the time of the murder or before?"

"I met her before."

"And since you say you met her before, did she ever confide in you about anything having to do with what she saw?"

"No."

"And why do you think she's not here in this courtroom today? Is it because you asked her not to come?"

"Objection, Your Honor," Clifton said.

"Can I ask you something?" I said.

"By all means, Mr. Calloway, the floor is yours."

"With all this evidence you say you have, where is my car? Where are my fingerprints in any of this? I've told you from the beginning, I did not murder Damien Price."

"But you did know him, correct?"

"I knew of him. We were never cool like that."

"Thank you, Mr. Calloway. I've heard enough," the judge interrupted. "You may step down now."

I looked over at him in confusion and looked at Clifton. When I sat back down at my table, the judge stared at us in silence.

"This witness that you speak of, Miss Valentine, is it? Did she agree to testify?"

"No, Your Honor. We have not been able to get the witness to agree to testify," the D.A. replied.

"Well then, if the only person you have that witnessed the murder won't testify, then you don't have much of a case, do you? I'm afraid I'm going to have to dismiss this case for lack of evidence. Mr. Calloway, I'm hereby dropping all charges against you. Court is dismissed," he said and slammed his gavel down.

Clifton and I stood and he turned to shake my hand.

"Thank you so much, man," I said as I gave him a quick hug.

"No problem. You're a free man now, Andreas. Let's just make sure you keep it that way, okay?"

"Okay. I will."

CHAPTER TWELVE
Raquel

I was pacing the bedroom floor back and forth, hoping and praying that Law was going to walk through those doors at any moment. I needed him to. After another twenty minutes of pacing, panicking, and praying, I heard the door open downstairs. I quickly ran out of the room, down the hall, and stood at the top of the steps. I let out a sigh of relief when I finally laid my eyes on him.

"How did everything go, baby?" I asked.

"You're lookin' at a free man." He smiled.

"Oh my God, Law! That's amazing. So they dropped everything?"

"Yeah. The judge saw the bullshit evidence they tried to present, heard Detective Mason's crazy ass story, then he heard mine, and he decided that since there was no witness, there wasn't enough evidence to take it to trial, and he dropped all the charges."

Law walked up the stairs and held me in his arms. I smiled and kissed his lips.

"Wow. That's amazing. I know you're so happy."

"Yeah, I am."

"So, what do you want to do to celebrate?"

"I'm actually gonna change out of these clothes, and Blaze and I are going to go pick up our mom. She agreed to move into the guest house, so we are going to get her settled in today. When she gets here though, I want the two of you to meet."

"Of course. I would love to meet your mom. Does she know that we are engaged?"

"No. Not yet. Only thing she knows about you so far is your name, but she wants to meet you."

"So, should I not wear my ring around her?"

"Nah. Wear it. We're going to tell her today—together."

"Okay."

Later that afternoon, Law came in the house and started yelling my name.

"I'm in the kitchen!" I yelled back.

Law appeared in the kitchen and walked over to me.

"She's here, and she's all settled in for the most part. Are you ready to go meet her now?"

"Yeah. I'm not gon' lie and say I'm not a little nervous, though. How do I look?"

"You look fine in what you have on. It's not a fashion show or nothin'. Relax."

I nodded and Law grabbed my hand. We walked outside of the main house and down the back walk way to the guest house. It was still pretty big, but it only had two bedrooms and two bathrooms inside. Law knocked on the door, and I slid my hand out of his and wiped the palms of my hands on the front of my pants. He looked back at me with a confused look on his face.

"I told you I'm nervous. My hands are sweating!" I whispered.

"Relax, Raquel," he told me.

My eyes darted back to the door when it opened. His mother and Blaze were standing there.

"You must be Raquel," his mother said.

"Hi. It's so nice to meet you, Mrs. Calloway."

Law and I walked in, and the four of us sat down in the living room.

"How are you feeling today, Ma? You need anything? You good?" Law asked.

"I'm fine. The two of you have already done enough."

"Okay." Blaze nodded.

"So, Raquel, how did you and my son meet?"

"Um, we ..."

"We met in South Beach at a club, Ma," Law interjected.

"Oh, I almost forgot. How did everything go with court?" she asked Law.

"Everything went fine. The judge dropped everything."

"I'm so happy to hear that."

"Yeah." He nodded. "Raquel, Blaze and I are going to leave the two of you alone for a little while so you can get to know each other better. You good with that?"

"Yeah. That's fine." I nodded as I rubbed my hands down my thighs again.

"She'll be fine. You two run along," his mother said.

Law gave me a quick peck on the lips, and then he and Blaze said their goodbyes to their mother. When they left, she turned back to me and smiled.

"So, Raquel, is that a ring I see on your finger?" she asked as she pointed to my hand.

"Yes." I beamed.

"When did this happen? Nobody told me!"

"Not too long ago. He told me we were going to tell you together, but surprise! I guess." I chuckled.

His mom laughed and shook her head.

"So, are you ready for your big day?" she asked me.

"Yes." I smiled. "I know it all seems fast, but I honestly can't wait to marry your son."

"I know he probably can't wait to marry you either. I know we're just meeting and everything, but I'm so happy he found you, Raquel. I really am. I see a big difference in him from the way he was with that other girl to the way he is with you. He's gentler, still firm, but gentle nonetheless."

The more time I spent around Law's mother, the more I

started to loosen up and actually relax. Although she was sick, she didn't let that get her down. I admired her for that.

"Thank you. That really means a lot to hear you say that and have your approval."

"So, do your parents know? Are they excited?"

"No. They don't know. I'm actually not that close with either of them. We talk here and there, but after their divorce, things just kind of got weird between us from there."

"I understand. Divorces can be messy."

"Yeah. I definitely don't want to go through that."

"I don't think you'll have to worry about that with Andreas. You know, the older he gets, the more he starts to remind me of his father when he was that age. Did he ever tell you the story about how his father and I got together?" she asked.

"No," I said, shaking my head.

"Well, I came from a crime family out of Georgia. My parents moved me and my sister here when we were babies to try and distance us from the family name and the legacy that went along with it. Although my father wanted to keep us away from all the drugs and the gangs, he still dabbled in it all from time to time. I grew up watching that, and hence, those were the types of men I started being attracted to. I liked the glitz and the money and the thrill, you know?"

"Right." I nodded. "How old were you when you met Law's father?"

"I was sixteen. We got married at eighteen and had Law's older brother, Asaad. Then came Andreas and Aston a few years later. Do you want to have babies with my son, Raquel?"

"To be honest, I haven't really thought much about kids or talked about it with him, but I love him. If it happens, I'll be fine with that. So to answer your question, yes. I do want to eventually have kids with him one day."

"How old are you now?" she asked.

"I'm twenty-two."

"Wow. I was much younger than you when I had my first child. I was only fifteen."

"Wait. I thought you said that you married his father when you were eighteen and had Wolfe then. I didn't know you were younger."

I studied Law's mother's face for an answer, but all she did was look at me with a blank stare.

"I'm sorry. Did I say something wrong?" I asked.

"No. I... um... I'm just tired. When I get tired, I get kind of confused. That's all. I'm going to go ahead and lay down for a bit. It's been a long day with all the moving and everything. We can finish this chat another time. It was nice meeting with you, Raquel."

"Uh... sure." I nodded and got up to leave. "It was nice meeting you as well."

I walked out of the guest house and closed the door behind me. I looked through the window and watched Law's mother sit in the same spot for five minutes. She smacked herself in the forehead once and then shook her head repeatedly. It became evident to me that she had a secret, and I knew if I hung around her long enough, I was going to find out exactly what it was.

* * *

When Blaze and I got back to the house, he told me that he had finally talked to the girl that he'd supposedly gotten pregnant and that she was coming over to the house.

"Coming over for what?"

"I want you to meet her. And you know? Feel her out," he said.

"You only want me to meet her?"

"I mean, she's cool, Law. I've been spending more time with her, and she's a real, genuine type of girl. She reminds me of Raquel."

"Yeah, but Raquel wasn't a stripper. Speaking of that, is she gon' keep doing that until she starts showing?"

"Nah. She's looking for another job now. I told her she had to quit that shit because it wasn't a good look."

"So, how she gettin' by until then? You payin' her bills already?" I asked.

"Nah. She good. She got money stacked up. She ain't asked me for a dime."

"Not yet."

Blaze rolled his eyes and shook his head.

"You tryna meet her or not?"

"Meet who?" Raquel asked as she walked up behind us.

"Heaven," Blaze told her.

"Is that her real name?" I asked.

"No, it's actually Nevaeh, which is Heaven spelled backwards. Your brother is just being difficult," Raquel told me.

"Oh."

"Is she coming over?" Raquel asked.

"Yeah. She should be here in the next twenty minutes or so."

"Okay. Cool. Maybe her, Camille, and I can all do something. I was supposed to meet up with her a few nights back, but I got sidetracked and never texted her back," Raquel said.

"No offense, Raquel, but I don't think I want Camille around Heaven."

"Why not?" she asked.

"Yeah. Why not?" I added.

"Because... I just don't."

"You might as well go on and spill the beans, Blaze, because I already know," Raquel said.

"Man, are you serious?" he said, sucking his teeth.

"What do you already know that I don't?" I asked her.

"I fucked her, aight?" Blaze blurted out.

"Nigggaaaa, what the fuck is wrong with you?" I asked, shaking my head.

It seemed like every time I turned around, Blaze was sticking his fucking dick in something. I couldn't do anything but shake my head.

"But don't worry about it. I already kinda let Camille know what was up with you and Nevaeh, so she will be cool. She's not that type of female," Raquel said.

"Yeah. Let's hope not," Blaze said as he walked out of the room.

About thirty minutes later, Blaze walked into the living room with Nevaeh trailing closely behind him.

"Hey, girl." Raquel smiled.

"Hey."

"Law, this is Nevaeh. Nevaeh, this is Law, my brother."

"Nice to meet you," I told her.

"Nice to meet you, too."

I sized her up from a distance. She was a cute girl and she may have even been a good person, but I couldn't let go of the fact that she reminded me of a gold digger. When Camille came downstairs, Raquel introduced her to Nevaeh then the three of them ran off together. I got up and walked into my office to roll a blunt. Blaze followed behind me and closed the door behind him.

"So, what you think?"

"I don't know. I mean, I only met her for two minutes. She seems nice, and Raquel likes her, but I think you still need to get a DNA test. Don't be stupid, nigga. I can see the shit all in your eyes."

Blaze shook his head at me and scrunched up his forehead.

"I know what the fuck I'm doing, nigga. You always tryna tell me what the fuck to do. You not Wolfe, and you not my fucking father!"

"Why you think that is, huh? You don't seem to make the best fucking decisions. And yeah, I'm not Wolfe, and I'm not our father, but I'm all you fucking got left, lil' nigga. Remember that shit. I'm the one that's got your fucking back at the end of the day. Her ass got your nose wide the fuck open, and I need you to come back down to earth and remember what the fuck is really real."

"Man, fuck you, Law. Ain't nobody say shit to you when you was walkin' around here frontin' like you ain't give a fuck about Raquel, knowing damn well you wanted her ass from the moment I brought her to you. You think you the only nigga around here that deserve a down ass bitch? Somebody that's gon' ride for them?"

"I'm not saying that. You too gone in the head to even hear what the fuck I'm trying to tell you, nigga. All I'm saying is make sure the baby is yours before you hand over everything to her. I ain't sayin' shit else but the facts. You met her at a strip club. She fucked you on the first night. You think it's because you got game or because that's what the fuck strippers do, nigga? Be smart!" I said, pointing at my temple.

"Get the fuck outta my face," Blaze said, shooing his hand at me.

"Or what, nigga? What the fuck are you gonna do, huh?"

"I'm tellin' you, Law, get the fuck out my face."

I stepped out from behind my desk, walked up to him, and looked him dead in the eyes.

"Or fucking what? Just because you my baby brother don't mean I won't fuck you up!"

Blaze shoved me and I shoved him back. Instead of charging after me like I thought he was going to do, he pulled his gun out on me.

"And just because you my fucking older brother don't mean I won't put a bullet in you either," he said as he held the gun to my temple.

I immediately had a flashback of when Wolfe pulled the gun out on Blaze when we were kids. I wasn't afraid, though. I just made sure not to make any sudden movements. That was just another moment where Blaze had made an irrational decision without thinking about the consequences. He may have been fast, but I would always be smarter.

"That's how you goin', Blaze? Big man, huh? Always quick to pull a fucking trigger and don't give a fuck about the consequences, huh?"

"Shut the fuck up, Law, or I swear to God," he said as his hand started to tremble out of anger.

That's when I knew I had him. His emotions had gotten the best of him, and I was going to capitalize on that. I quickly reached behind my back, pulled out my gun, and put it to his temple.

"I'm my brother's keeper, right? Right, nigga!" I yelled.

Blaze didn't move. We both stood there playing Russian Roulette with each other's lives and staring each other down. We were both a bullet away from losing it all, but neither of us gave a fuck. It was clear to me that my brother had forgot who the fuck had his best interest at heart. It was me, and it was always gonna be me first. Blaze was breathing heavily with his face balled up like a piece of loose-leaf paper when he lowered his gun.

"Stay the fuck outta my business from here on out, and I'll do the same with yours," he said as he walked out of the room.

CHAPTER THIRTEEN

Raquel

I woke up the next day with Law's mother on my mind. I couldn't let go of the conversation we had. She seemed like a sharp woman who would never forget a detail, especially about her own life. I just wanted to know why her story switched up and why she acted so distant after I called her out on it.

"Hey. Where are you going?" Law asked me.

"I'm just going to check on your mom to see if she needs anything."

Before I heard a response, I was out the door and headed down to the guest house. I knocked gently on the door and waited for his mother to open it. A few minutes later, she came to the door.

"Raquel, it's early. What are you doing here? Is everything okay?"

"Yes. Everything is fine. I just came to check on you to see if you needed anything."

"No. I'm okay."

"Um... okay. I know this is random and even really awkward, but I was hoping we could finish our conversation from yesterday."

"And what part of that conversation would you like to finish?" she asked.

"The part about you being fifteen when you had your first child. That wasn't a mistake. It was the truth, wasn't it?" I asked.

159

"Come inside, Raquel."

I slowly walked inside and sat down with her at the kitchen table.

"What do you really want to know?" she asked.

"The truth. Did you have another baby before Wolfe, Law, and Blaze came along?"

I searched her eyes for a moment. I could see them getting glossier by the second, and I felt bad for bringing up old, and possibly even painful memories.

"I did."

"And it wasn't with their father?"

"Remember when I told you I used to fall for hustlers when I was younger? Well, there was one in particular that I was completely in love with. His name was Dominique Price."

I put my hand over my mouth as my eyes widened. I was just hoping that it was a coincidence that his last name was Price, but I kept listening.

"I had my first child before I met Law's father. I was only fifteen back then, and I was secretly dating Dominique. He took my virginity, and I got pregnant not too long after that. He was an older gang member. I think he was about nineteen at the time, and I was underage. So, once he found out I was pregnant, he told me that he didn't want the baby."

"So, what did you do?"

"I was so in love at the time and dumb. I thought that he would eventually change his mind, and I was right because he did by the time I was five months. I kept the baby, and Dominique told me that after I had him he was going to take him and raise him until I turned eighteen, and then we could be together without the risk of him going to jail. Like a fool, I believed him. The night I gave birth, he took my baby and left Miami."

"Oh my God. I'm so sorry."

"I didn't know what to do. I was distraught. There I was, thinking that I was going to get my happily ever after with Dominique, and he left me with nothing. I was depressed for a whole year. I don't know if it was postpartum or what, but things didn't start looking up for me until I met Law's father when I was sixteen going on seventeen. I really started feeling complete again when we got married, and I had Law's older brother."

"Was your baby a boy or a girl?"

"A boy."

"Did you ever see your first son again?"

"I didn't see Damien again until I was twenty. Assad was already two years old."

"Wait... your first son was Damien Price? Does Law know that?" I asked.

Law's mother sighed and shook her head.

"Nobody knew but their father. I'm the reason why the Calloway and Price families are still rivals today."

"Oh shit," I mumbled.

"I thought I would take this secret to my grave, but my heart just can't take it anymore," she said as she wiped her eyes. "It was something that just spiraled out of control from the moment Dominique came back to Miami with Damien. He found me, and I told him that I was married. Once he saw that I had a family and another child, he decided that he wanted me back. I told my husband, and the two of them had many showdowns over the years, but both vowed to never hurt each other out of respect for me. All of that went out the window when my husband was killed."

"You think he had something to do with it?"

"I don't think. I know."

"Well, is he still alive?"

"Last I heard, he was. But I'm not sure," she said, shaking her head.

"You have to tell Law and Blaze about Damien. This could put an end to everything between them and Damien's two younger brothers," I told her.

"I can't," she said, shaking her head. "It would kill them, and they'd never forgive me. I still haven't forgiven myself after all these years."

"Do you really want to lose another son over this secret?" I asked.

"You just don't understand, Raquel. I get that you're trying to help, but it isn't your place. Some things are best left buried in the past. Okay?"

"I hear you, but..."

"But nothing, Raquel. If you want to make it in this family, in this lifestyle, you're going to have to learn how to hold onto secrets... sometimes for life. You hear me? You are not going to tell Law or anybody else what I just told you. This stays between you and I."

She stared at me with a cold look in her eyes, and I simply nodded at her. She was right. I had been holding onto secrets left and right since I came to Miami. Hers was just another one added to the pile.

"Okay. I won't tell him... but I still think you should."

I got up and walked out of the guest house in a huff. I didn't know whether to tell anybody or just keep it to myself like his mother had told me to. My thoughts stopped when my phone vibrated in my pocket. It was Derrick. I rolled my eyes and answered before I walked back into the house.

"What do you want?" I answered.

"I just want to talk."

"I think we talked about everything the last time I saw you, Derrick. What else is there?"

"So, you're really doing this, Raquel? You're really getting married?"

"Yes! What part of that don't you get, Derrick?"

"I'm just trying to stop you from making a mistake. This is a big mistake, Raquel."

"Why? Because I won't be walking down the aisle to marry you? Is that why you don't want me to get married?"

"No. It's not that. I just don't think you know what you're

getting yourself into, Raquel. Do you even love him? Do you know him well enough to marry him and spend the rest of your life with him?"

"Oh, like I thought I knew you, right? Leave me the fuck alone, Derrick. I'm done with you. There's no more us, okay? Don't call my phone anymore. Just go back home! Leave Miami before you get hurt," I said and hung up.

* * *

Blaze

I hadn't spoken to Law since the standoff we had in his office. The house was cold when we didn't speak, and everyone could feel it. I felt bad for overreacting like I did, but I needed him to know I was an adult, and I wasn't a child. He needed to learn to let me fly out on my own and live my life the way I wanted to. He couldn't protect me from everything forever.

"Hey," I said as I walked outside and saw him standing by his car.

"What's up?"

"Look, man, I just wanted to apologize for the shit that went down between us. You know I would never do nothin' to hurt you. I was just mad, and I felt like you were trying to be on some holier than thou type shit," I told him.

"It's cool. You a grown ass man. I guess it's time I stop seeing you as just my little brother and give you the space you need to continue to grow, but I'm gonna be there for you no matter what."

"It's all love," I said as I dapped him up and pulled him into a hug.

"Bet." He nodded and patted my back.

"So, you ready for this wedding?"

"I guess." He shrugged.

"What you mean *you guess?* It's gonna be different this time, my nigga. It's gotta be."

"I hope you're right."

"You just gotta think about all the good shit that's about to happen. We finally got those Price niggas in check, and you about to marry a girl that's down for you. It don't get no better than that."

"Yeah. I know. What about you? You ready to be a father?"

"I don't know. I probably won't know until it's here, and I have to deal with it."

"You'll be alright. Have you told Ma yet?"

"Nah. I'll tell her as soon as I get the DNA test done."

"So, you are going to do it?"

"Yeah. We found out we can get it done any time after eight weeks. All it is, is a blood sample from the both of us, and I'll know for sure if the kid is mine. Then I can move forward."

"I'm proud of you." Law nodded.

"Thanks." I smiled. "I'm proud of you, too. Shit is finally starting to come together for us."

"Yeah. Let's just hope it stays that way."

* * *

Nashiya

I called Dallas over to my hotel and told him that I wanted to see him. Truth was, I was in need of a good dick down, and I needed to plant another seed in his head. I found out that the charges were dropped against Law, which pissed me off, and I didn't know if Derrick had followed through with my advice on pursuing Raquel harder. But if that didn't work, I wanted to make sure I had a plan C in place. I didn't give a fuck what I had to do, I was going to make sure that Law didn't marry that bitch. If I couldn't have him, she wasn't going to have him either.

When Dallas knocked on the door, I answered wearing a black lace bra and panty set.

"Oh shit," he said as he smiled and licked his lips. "That's why you called me over, Bird?"

"Yup," I said, flashing him a seductive look.

I pulled him in the room and dropped to my knees to unbuckle his pants and pull them down. I pushed my hair to the side and started sucking his dick. I reached around my back to unhook my bra and exposed my breasts. I made sure to get his dick nice and wet before I put it in between my breasts and let him titty fuck me. I put my head down and took his dick back in my mouth and started sucking him without using my hands.

"Yeah. That's it, Bird. Suck that dick."

"Mmmm... Your dick tastes so fucking good."

He put both hands on the back of my head and thrust

forward so that his dick touched my tonsils. I sucked him so hard my cheeks started hurting.

"You know what you doin' with that dick, don't you?"

"Mmhm," I said as I continued to suck.

Dallas pulled me to my feet and bent me over the side of the bed. He pushed my head down into the pillows and slid his dick inside me.

"Mmm, shit," he groaned.

"Yessss! Smack my ass, D!" I yelled as I turned my neck to look back at him.

He grabbed my right arm and pulled it behind my back then stuck his finger in my asshole.

"Mmmm... shit!"

"Daddy knows just how you like it."

He pushed me down further so that my body was laying parallel to the bed and drove all his weight into my back to keep me from moving. Then he climbed on the bed and turned me over on my side. I pulled my panties off, spread my legs, and started rubbing my pussy. Dallas stood there watching me and smiling. I rubbed on my nipples and smiled.

"Damn. Look at that pussy glistening."

"Just for you." I smirked.

"Just for me, huh?"

"Yup."

Dallas slid back inside me while I laid on my side.

"Ooooh shit," I said as I rubbed my clit faster.

Dallas held my leg in the air and drilled into me and wrapped his hands around my neck from behind. I reached back and spread my cheeks so he could thrust deeper inside me. He was so deep inside me I could feel his balls slap against the bottom of my ass.

"Spread them cheeks for daddy, Bird. Mm, shit! Just like that. Damn, I love you, girl," he mumbled.

I froze for a moment when I heard the L word. I didn't expect him to say it, especially not during sex. I used to love him. I used to love Law, too. I just didn't know what love was anymore. Dallas kept pumping into me, but I was too out of it to even enjoy the sex anymore, and I wanted him to hurry up and finish.

"I want you to cum, Dallas," I moaned.

"You want me to cum, huh?"

"Mmm... yeah. I do."

He sped up the pace to fuck me harder until he came. He pulled me close to him as we laid on the bed trying to settle our breathing.

"Damn," he said as he slid out of me and wiped his forehead.

"Damn is right."

"Oh, and don't act like I didn't hear you say you loved me back either."

I sighed and got up to go to the bathroom.

"Shut up, Dallas. You're being dramatic."

"I'm for real, Shiya. What? You don't love me?" he asked.

"C'mon now. ou know I do, but..."

"Aw hell. There's a but. It's never good when there's a but with you."

"I need you to do something for me."

"What is it this time?" he asked.

"I want him dead," I said as I walked out of the bathroom and stood in front of him.

"What? Who?" he asked, looking at me crazy.

I brushed my hand against the side of his cheek and rested my thumb underneath his chin.

"I said I want Law dead this time."

CHAPTER FOURTEEN

Raquel

I
t was the night before my wedding, and Camille and I were sitting in the house talking when she had the bright idea to start tearing up the kitchen.

"What are you doing?" I asked as I walked in behind her as she had her nose in the pantry.

"Since you don't wanna go out and have a real bachelorette party, we're gonna bake up a storm in here! You remember when we used to bake cookies every time we had a sleepover?"

"Yeah. I do."

"Well, welcome to 2002, bitch." She laughed as she looked through the freezer. "Wait. Where are the damn cookies?"

"I don't know. I've never made them here before."

"So, y'all ain't got no damn cookies in here? What about brownie mix or cake mix?"

I shrugged.

"I guess not."

"What the fuck, Raquel?"

"Sorry! Look, make a list of everything that you want, and I'll run out to the store and get it. When I get back, we can have the bake off of the century."

"I can come with you if you want."

"Nah. It's okay. What do we need?"

"Let's see... milk, eggs, brownie mix, frozen cookie dough... anything else?"

"Okay... milk, eggs, cookie dough, and brownies. Got it." I nodded. "I'll be right back!"

I ran upstairs, grabbed a twenty-dollar bill from off the dresser along with my phone and my car keys. I drove to the grocery store and parked in the lot. I didn't even care if I was in between the lines or not. I planned to be in and out in no time. My phone rang as soon as I walked into the store. I looked down and saw that it was Derrick once again. I rolled my eyes and pressed the decline button to ignore it. His ass was acting super pressed, and I didn't understand why. He didn't give a fuck about me when we were together, but now that I was close to marrying someone else, he wanted to be all on my line.

> Derrick: Raquel. My flight leaves out of Miami tomorrow morning. Can I please just see you on more time before I go?

> Raquel: What part of we're done don't you understand? Leave me alone!

Instead of responding to my message, he called me again.

"You're really starting to piss me off, Derrick!" I said into the receiver as I pushed the cart around the store.

"Turn around."

"What?" I said as I slowly looked over my shoulder.

Derrick was standing at the end of the aisle with his phone in one hand and a frozen dinner in the other. The sight of him scared me. I didn't know if he had resorted to stalking me or what, but I wasn't feeling it. I left the cart in the middle of the aisle and walked toward him.

"Are you fucking stalking me now?" I asked.

"No, no! It's not like that. My hotel is right around the corner from here. I just came to grab something quick to eat tonight. I didn't want to spend any extra money at the restaurant in the hotel. How are you?"

"I'm annoyed."

"I'm sorry... I didn't mean to. I just... I just wanted to see you one more time before I left, seeing as the next time I see you, you'll probably be a married woman, right?"

"Exactly. Now if you don't mind, I'd like to grab the rest of my groceries in peace and go on about my business," I told him.

Derrick nodded, and I turned to walk back to my cart and continue shopping. I got the rest of the things and went through self-checkout so that I could head back home. I carried my bags out to the parking lot and unlocked the car. As soon as I bent down to put the bags in the back seat, I heard a vehicle pull up beside me. The door opened, and before I could turn around, I was grabbed from behind. Someone pulled me in the running vehicle, backed out, and sped off.

My heart was racing just like the first time I'd been kidnapped, except I could see everything. I looked up and saw a man in all black driving the car, and Dallas in the passenger seat.

"Dallas? What the fuck is going on?" I asked.

"Shut up and lay back," he said as he put his gun to my head.

I slowly put my shaking hands up in the air and closed my mouth. Dallas held the gun in my direction until the car pulled up to an abandoned warehouse and the engine shut off.

"Get out," he demanded.

I reluctantly got out and followed him inside the warehouse. When I got inside, the first person I saw was Nashiya standing there with her arms folded.

"Nashiya, w—what are you doing here?" I asked as my lip trembled.

"Never underestimate a bitch with a plan, Raquel. I told you the last time I saw you, you hadn't seen anything yet, didn't I?"

"What the fuck is going on? What do y'all want from me?" I asked.

"Your life, bitch," Shiya said.

Dallas pulled me by my arm and pushed me down into a chair.

"Dallas, you don't have to do this," I cried.

"Oh, shut the fuck up, bitch! You thought I was just gonna sit here and watch you marry Law and run off into the fucking sunset together? Huh? Hell no!" Shiya yelled out before he could say anything.

"I mean, you gotta give it to her. The shit was perfect," he said as he released the safety on his gun.

"Dallas, please!"

"Pull the trigger, D," Shiya told him.

I closed my eyes and prepared to take my last breath when Dallas stopped.

"Hold up. Did you hear that?" Dallas asked Nashiya.

"Hear what?" she asked.

"Over there by the door. Go check it out."

"What the fuck are you doing here?" she yelled as she walked over to the door.

When Nashiya came back, she was pushing Derrick into the area where Dallas and I were standing.

"Shit. What the fuck are you doing here?" Shiya asked as she pushed Derrick again.

"Derrick? What the fuck are you doing here?" I asked. "Wait a minute. Are you in on this shit with them?"

"No, Raquel! I swear! I followed you here when I saw you get pulled into the car. Nashiya, what is going on?"

"You know this nigga?" Dallas asked Nashiya.

"I—I met him once at a bar."

"He's my ex-fiancé," I told Dallas. "And she knew that!"

"Hold up. You two know each other?" Derrick asked in confusion.

"Shut up, and sit the fuck down," Dallas said, pointing his gun at Derrick. "I'm the one asking the fucking questions here."

Derrick slowly lifted his hands and sat down beside me.

"Now, somebody better tell me what the fuck is going on before I blast every fucking body in this bitch."

"I knew you were going to be a problem from day one," Shiya

said as she looked me up and down. "Dallas, give me the gun. I want to shoot this bitch myself."

"Wait! Dallas, please don't!" I yelled out.

"Don't what?" he said, raising his voice.

"Don't shoot!"

"Give me one good reason I shouldn't!"

"Because Law was Damien's brother!" I blurted out.

In order to save my own life, I decided to spill the secret that Law's mother told me to keep. I didn't know if it was going to work, but it was the only card I had left in my hand to play.

"What?" he asked.

"I said... he was Damien's brother," I told him as I tried to slow my heart rate down.

"Stop lying, bitch," Shiya said. "Dallas, give me the gun!"

"I'm not lying. I have proof. Living proof! Just trust me!"

"Who?" Dallas asked.

"Their mother. Law, Wolfe, Blaze, and Damien were half-brothers. Damien was the oldest. Their mother had him with your father when she was just a teenager."

"And you expect me to believe you just like that?"

"It's what I know. I swear to God! I don't have any reason to lie to you right now."

"What the fuck, Dallas!" Shiya yelled as she reached for his gun.

Dallas pulled the gun away from her, and the gun went off. I screamed as I watched Shiya's body hit the ground.

"Oh shit!" Derrick yelled as he scrambled backward.

Dallas looked down at Nashiya's body with a bullet hole through her chest and then looked up at me. He dropped the gun on the ground as his hand trembled.

"Man, fuck!" he screamed out. "I didn't fucking mean to do that shit!"

"It's okay. We know you didn't. It was an accident. Please, just let us go. Just let us go back home, and I swear we won't tell anybody about what we saw here tonight. Isn't that right, Derrick?" I said.

"Yeah. I swear I won't say shit," Derrick said, shaking his head.

"Oh, I know you won't because you're going to help me get rid of her body, and so is she," Dallas said, pointing to me.

"No. I'll help you. Just... just leave him out of it. He doesn't know shit about anything."

"Whether you think he knows shit or not, he's in this now, Raquel, and there's only one way he's getting out. Is that what you want? To help me bury two fucking bodies or one?"

"No," I said, shaking my head.

"That's what I thought," he said as he turned his focus to Derrick. "Drag her ass over onto that tarp and roll her up. Raquel, you check her pockets for anything that could identify her."

I wiped my face and crawled on my knees to check Shiya's pockets. My ears were still ringing from the gunshot. I slowly slid my hand inside her pockets. There was nothing in them but lint and a tube of lipstick. I watched Dallas walk over and stand over her body.

"Hold her mouth open," he told me.

"What?"

"I said hold her fucking mouth open!"

I hesitantly parted Shiya's lips as Dallas stood over her. Her turned to look at Derrick and pointed behind him.

"Hand me the jug of bleach in the corner."

Derrick hesitantly handed Dallas the jug of bleach, and we both watched him pour it into her mouth and all over her body. I turned my head away from him. Once the jug was empty, he looked at Derrick.

"Help me wrap her up so we can put her in the trunk and then both of you get in the car."

Derrick helped Dallas carry Nashiya's dead body out of the warehouse and put her in the trunk. I looked around and saw Dallas talking to the guy who had drove us to the warehouse. He patted him on the back, and he went into the warehouse. Then we all got in the car, and Dallas sped off. He stopped when we got to a private dock a few miles away. There was a motor boat attached to it.

"Get the fuck out, and put her body on the boat."

"Dallas, we don't have to do this," I cried.

"Shut the fuck up, Raquel! It was supposed to be her standing here beside me burying you, not the other fucking way around, but I could still kill you. Just fucking try me!"

I nodded slowly as my nostrils flared, trying to hold back more tears. Derrick got out of the car, and Dallas popped the trunk. They carried Nashiya's body out of the trunk and walked it over to the edge of the dock. I followed slowly behind them. I was hoping Dallas would slip up somehow so that I could get his gun or push him in the water, but he didn't. Truth was, I was too scared to make any sudden movements. All I could focus on was surviving.

Dallas got in the boat first, and Derrick passed him Shiya's body.

"Damn, this bitch is getting heavier," he said as he dropped her body on the floor of the boat.

Derrick climbed in and then I did. Dallas started the engine, and we took off, going a few hundred feet from the dock. He slowed down the boat, and I listened to the engine settle down.

"Toss her overboard," he told Derrick.

Derrick looked at Dallas and then looked back at me.

"Just do what he says, Derrick," I told him as I shook my head.

Derrick stood up and lifted Shiya's body in his arms and then tossed it into the water. The three of us watched it sink until we could no longer see any of the tarp. Derrick sat down, and Dallas headed back towards the dock. When we pulled back up, we got off the boat one by one—first Derrick then Dallas and me. As Derrick walked back to the car, Dallas lifted his arm and pointed his gun at Derrick's back.

"Dallas, no!" I yelled as he pulled the trigger.

I screamed as Derrick's body fell forward onto the dock, and he hit his head.

"Oh my God!" I yelled as I ran toward him. "What the fuck did you just do?"

"Calm down. I didn't kill him."

I touched the side of Derrick's neck to check for a pulse. He was still alive for the moment.

"Why did you shoot him? He has nothing to do with this! What if he dies?"

"He won't."

"What if he does? That's two murders on your hands, Dallas! Two!"

"If he don't die, Raquel, I'll make him wish he was dead. What do you think he'll choose when I'm done with him, huh? He's already seen what I'm capable of."

"We can't just leave him here."

"Somebody will find him and take his ass to the hospital. The good thing is he'll be alive, and he'll be too scared to talk. Does that help your little conscience now? Get in the fucking car."

"Dallas..."

"Get in the car, or I'm going to put a bullet in you to match his."

I walked over and got back in the car just as Dallas pressed his foot all the way down on the gas pedal and sped off. The car didn't slow down until we pulled back into the parking lot of the grocery store where my car was.

"Remember, this is our little secret, Raquel. I spared your fucking life. Don't make me regret my decision, or I will come and find you," he warned me.

I looked at him and screwed my face up. Yeah, he had saved my life, but at what cost? In my eyes, Dallas Price was a fucking monster.

"And you make sure you scrub those fucking fingers good, too. Don't want bloody residue under your nails on your wedding day."

I swallowed hard and watched as he hit the button to take the car off child lock so I could get out of the car. When I opened the door, I cut my eyes at him and ran back to my car and pulled off. I sped all the way back to the house. I didn't stop until I got in the shower to scrub all of Shiya's dried blood off my body. I didn't know if I was happy she was dead and out of my life for good or scared of myself for what I'd help Dallas do to get rid of her body to save my own ass.

I couldn't believe all of that had transpired the night before my wedding. I stepped out of the shower and wrapped the towel around my wet body. I almost jumped out of my skin when I heard a knock on the bathroom door.

"Raqi? Is that you?" Camille asked.

I let out a loud huff of air and unlocked the door.

"Hey," I said.

"Hey... is everything okay? You were supposed to come right back here after you ran to the store so we could bake cookies and shit... Did you get the stuff?" she asked.

I looked at Camille and shook my head.

"Yeah. I'm sorry, something came up, and I got side tracked."

"Well, where are the cookies?"

"I—I must've left them in the trunk," I whispered.

"Are you sure everything is okay, Raquel?" she asked.

I shook my head. I could feel the tears building up in the back of my eyes. I pulled Camille close to me and hugged her tight as I started crying.

"Oh my God, Raquel. What's wrong?" she asked.

"I'm scared, Camille. I'm so fucking scared," I cried.

"Scared of what? To get married? Is that it? Are you having cold feet?"

"No, no. That's not it." I sniffed.

"Then what is it? Talk to me."

I pulled Camille into the bathroom and locked the door behind me. I walked over to the shower and turned it on as well as the bathroom fan so no one could hear our conversation.

"Okay... What the fuck is going on, Raquel? You're making me nervous."

"Camille... if I really tell you what's going on, you have to swear on your life you won't tell anybody."

"I swear I won't, Raquel. You have my word."

"Because if you do, it really could be the difference between life or death for me and... a lot of other people," I told her.

"Like I said, you have my word."

I took a deep breath and then exhaled deeply.

"You remember Law's ex, Shiya, right?"

"Yeah, the bitch you won't let me fight. What about her?"

"She's dead, Camille," I said as I sniffed.

"Did you kill her, Raquel?"

"No," I said, shaking my head. "It wasn't me."

"Okay. If it wasn't you, then who was it?"

I shook my head as fresh tears rolled down my cheeks.

"I don't know what to do, Camille."

"What is the problem, Raquel? You didn't kill her. Did Law do it? Are you trying to cover for him?"

"No, he doesn't know... and then Derrick... poor Derrick!" I sobbed.

"Hold up. Derrick? What does he have to do with any of this?"

"Somebody else killed her, and they made me and Derrick help them dispose of her body."

"Wait. What! What the fuck!" she yelled.

"Shh! Lower your fucking voice! I told you, you can't say a motherfucking thing, or that's it for Derrick and me!"

"Are you gonna tell Law?"

"I don't know," I said, shaking my head.

"Raquel, are you kidding me? You have to tell him! You have to tell him right fucking now! He's the only one who can get you out of this shit!"

"I know, but..."

"But nothing, Raquel. Go find your fucking phone, and call your man!"

"It's not that simple!"

"Why isn't it?" she asked.

"Because I know something that could tear his whole world apart. That's the only reason they let me live. That was supposed to be my dead body being disposed of today, Camille. I'm not even supposed to be alive right now," I cried.

Camille reached out to hug me and rubbed my back.

"It's okay, Raquel. Don't worry about it. We'll figure it out, okay? For now, I'll move however you wanna move. Your secret is safe with me."

CHAPTER FIFTEEN

Raquel

It was the day of my wedding, a day I never thought I'd see come to fruition, but I felt like shit. I was a nervous wreck and barely had gotten any sleep the night before. I knew I needed to tell Law that the real reason his family hated the Price family was because of what happened with his mother over twenty years ago. Damien was his half brother, and his mother never told him about it. I also needed to tell him that Shiya was dead, and I helped get rid of her body.

"Are you okay?" Camille asked me as she reached out and grabbed my hand.

"No. I'm not. I have to tell him, Camille. This marriage is going to be based off lies and secrets if I don't, and I don't want that."

"Like I told you last night, I'll follow your moves. Whatever you choose to do is fine with me."

I nodded as I inhaled and exhaled deeply. I closed my eyes to say a quick prayer and then walked down the aisle. I was still a mess. My hands were clammy and shaking, and my stomach was doing backflips. I looked at Camille, Blaze, Nevaeh, and Law's mother. Everyone was smiling at me. I looked down the aisle at Law and time stopped. In that moment, he was everything I'd ever wanted him to be and more. I never would've thought that after all that I went through after coming down to Miami, it would end with me finding the love of my life. That thought alone made me smile. As soon as I made it down to him, he stretched out his hands to me. My hands shook as I placed them in his.

"Are you nervous?" he whispered to me.

"You can't tell?"

"Don't be."

Before I could get another word out, the preacher started the ceremony. I tuned out after I heard the first couple words and focused all of my attention on Law. I snapped back to reality when I heard him mention my name.

"Raquel, do you take Andreas to be your lawfully wedded husband?"

I looked Law in the eyes and then looked down at my hands.

"Law, there's something I need to tell you first."

"What is it?"

"I ..."

"Can it wait until after the ceremony?" he asked, cutting me off.

I exhaled slowly and nodded.

"Yeah... um... I guess it can."

"Raquel, what is your answer?" the preacher asked me.

"I do."

"And do you, Andreas, take Raquel to be your lawfully wedded wife?"

Law looked me in my eyes and smiled.

"I..."

Pow. Pow. Pow.

My mouth gaped open as I watched Law's body fly back into the pulpit. I let out a horrific scream as I dropped down to my knees, trying to shield my body and his from the bullets flying around inside the church. People were screaming, running, and Blaze was shooting back. The preacher was hit, and he fell backward into one of the choir chairs. After what felt like an eternity, all the shooting stopped. I heard shell casings rolling around on the floor and people screaming and crying.

"Oh my God!" I screamed.

I laid there, staring at Law as he blinked slowly.

"C'mon, baby. Stay with me, baby. Stay with me, okay?" I told him. "You can't leave me, Law! Please! Please don't leave me!"

I grabbed his hand to squeeze it, hoping he would squeeze mine back, but instead, he closed his eyes. I was completely distraught. It only took one bullet to ruin our happily ever after with no signs of it coming back.

"Law, no! Please don't do this, baby! Please don't!" I cried.

I stared down at him with his eyes closed, and within a few seconds, Law was gone.

* * *

Law

"Do not be afraid of those who kill the body but cannot kill the soul. Rather, be afraid of the one who can destroy both soul and body in hell."- Matthew 10:28

I came into the world drenched in blood, and I was going out the same way. All I could hear were muffled screams underneath the loud thumping of my heartbeat. Although it was loud, it was slowing down with every gasp of air I took. I laid there with my eyes closed, asking the Lord to forgive me for my sins. My biggest sin of all was lying to the people I loved the most and faking my death.

Don't ask me how I knew that something was going to go

wrong the day of my wedding, but I made sure I was prepared. No sooner than Raquel said I do, those mothafucking Price niggas showed up, and I stood there, ready and waiting. As soon as the first bullet pierced my chest, I fell back. It stung like hell, but it wasn't anything compared to what it would've really felt like if I didn't have on my bulletproof vest. The last phase of my plan was set in motion when my body hit the ground. I was going to lay back and wait for those niggas to slip. After all, they say pressure bursts pipes, right? And you better believe when the time came, it was going to be a bloody fucking massacre.

TO BE CONTINUED...

Afterword

Readers,

Thanks for following along with me on my literary journey so far. Also, thank you for reading the second installment of the *In the Arms of a Savage* series. Got a second to leave a review? If you've made it this far, I hope you'll consider taking a minute to tell me what you thought about the book. I thoroughly enjoy reading them! Why does this matter? I'm always striving to attract new readers and retain current ones, and reviews are one of the easiest ways to attract readers. If you loved the book, tell a friend, and most importantly, let me know!

Thanks so much,

K.L. Hall

Other books by K.L. Hall:

Make Mine a Gangsta: The Patton Brothers Book One

Gimme a Gangsta: The Patton Brothers Book Two

In the Arms of a Savage 1-3

Short Reads + Novellas:

Bi-Curious: An Erotic Tale

Bi-Curious 2: Tastes Like Candy

A Savage Calloway Christmas *(Christmas novella to the In the Arms of a Savage Series)*

Lovin' the Alpha of the Streets: A Valentine's Day Novella *(Valentine's Day novella to the Fallin' for the Alpha of the Streets Series)*

Awakened: A Paranormal Romance

As Long as You Stay Down

Solace in Seven

Solace II: The Final Cut

Something Bleu

Something Borrowed

Something New

The Knight Before Christmas: A Potomac Falls Short

I'll Be Home for Christmas: A Potomac Falls Short Book II

Triggered: A Potomac Falls Novella

Wasted Off You: A Friends to Lovers Novella

Because You Don't Know My Name: A Potomac Falls Novella

Will You Say My Name: A Potomac Falls Novella Book Two

Remember My Name: A Potomac Falls Novella Book Three

Every Thug Needs a Lady: A Lady and the Tramp Retelling

Ten Things I Hate About Lovin' You: An Enemies to Lovers Novella

In Exchange: An Urban Thriller

T.A.N.: An Erotic Novella

Children's Books:

Princess for Hire

Princess Twinkle Toes & the Missing Magic Sneakers

Little One, Change the World

Adjust Your Crown: A Self-Love Coloring Book for Children of Color

Non-Fiction:

Authors are a Business: The Booked & Busy Course Mini Book

Connect With Me on Social Media:

Facebook: K.L. Hall https://goo.gl/yGP59B

Twitter: @authorklhall

Instagram: @authorklhall

Website: www.authorklhall.com

Sign up for my mailing list to stay up to date with new releases, giveaways, and more here: goo.gl/l6IMUp

www.ingramcontent.com/pod-product-compliance
Lightning Source LLC
Chambersburg PA
CBHW022152240626
47153CB00007B/2633